CHALLENGE

By

PHILIP E BARTOW

CONTENTS

PREFACE

CHALLENGE is a fictional adventure rooted in the real-life encounters and experiences of the author. The technical descriptions of climbing techniques from rock faces to handholds, from belay activity to prussik knots functionality are as instructive as they are practical, if not entertaining.

Sequences dealing with geology, geography, topology even engineering and project planning likewise are all reality based. The author's background working for an exploration mining company in the state of Alaska and survival experiences using innovative materials and personal ingenuity evolve from engineering academic teaching and consultancy in management as well as spear heading a professional outdoor challenge organization.

The management conflicts in the story are based on a real-life company in transition. The characters are developed within the story in such a way as to induce the reader to wonder if they are truly fictional.

CHAPTER 1
CHALLENGE

Only one of the two climbers could be seen 1,500 feet up the face of a granite cliff from the valley floor. The other climber was higher up, sitting on a ledge while pulling up the slack in the rope each time the person below him moved upward. The climber disappeared from the view of the campers in the valley as he reached the ledge.

"Thanks for the belay, boss. Belay off," Juan Martinez said as he stepped up onto the ledge and shook the rope away from his feet. They were near the top of a large granite monolith at the head end of an inlet north of Vancouver, B.C. The hemlock forest below looked like a green carpet stretching to the sound. The breeze carried the scent of salt mixed with pine. Brown crusty lichen covered the rock in patches. Juan scraped some loose with his foot and watched it drift downward. "Wow. That is a long way down."

The lichen disappeared. "Enjoying yourself?" he asked his companion.

"Rock feels good after a month on ice," Roy Graham replied as he took a deep breath, sucking in the thin air. "I've gotten used to lower altitude. This thin air is invigorating. Another three hundred feet to the top. Once we get above this overhang we have one easy face."

Roy studied the route above him for a few seconds consciously noting small indentations, cracks and small flakes casting microscopic shadows. Subconsciously he was building a schedule of moves, a mental model of the path he would take up the cliff, and playing it back like a movie. He gazed at the grey and black flecks of granite until a silent understanding of mind interplaying with body merged. He was ready.

The warning shrill of a startled eagle pierced the quiet air. The bird swept away from the cliff higher up, quickly rose in an expanding circle then disappeared behind the rock above them.

"We will follow that narrow crack running up to the overhang. There are some good horizontal flakes. It should be interesting." He reset the belay anchor and handed the rope to Juan.

Roy started to climb up the crack. It was just wide enough to jam the toes of his shoes into. He hung on by putting his hand in the crack and making a fist. He ascended the crack thirty feet as if he were climbing a ladder. The crack ran up to the bottom of the overhang that jutted out over the valley floor like the ceiling of a room. The crack ended where another thin crack ran horizontally along the base where the ceiling and wall joined.

Roy removed a spoon-shaped titanium piton from a harness of other rock climbing items hanging from his shoulder and slipped it into the horizontal crack. He carefully took a hammer from the harness. Still hanging on with a fist clenched in the vertical crack, he drove the piton into the thin crack. Each time he hit the piton the sound of the vibrating metal increased in pitch. When the ringing stopped and it sounded and felt like he was hitting rock he knew he had a solid anchor that would hold him if he fell. Replacing the hammer on the harness he removed an oval-shaped carabineer, connected it to the piton, then snapped the climbing rope into the carabineer.

Juan could now stop Roy from below if he should fall.

Roy hung onto the carabineer with his left hand. Leaning out from the wall and stretching he was able to place the fingertips of his right hand on a small flake on the outer edge of the the overhang. The tactile sense of tough weathered fingers on cold, sharp granite felt reassuringly secure. He let go of the carabineer with his left hand and gently swung out, hanging by three fingers of one hand over a fifteen-hundred-foot void. Roy placed two fingers of his left hand on the flank and with a grunt he chinned up quickly. With his momentum still moving upward, he let go with his left-hand fingers and reached up to a small but secure hold with his left hand. As smoothly as a choreographed dance he removed the fingers of his right hand from the small flake, now hanging from his left hand and pulling up, placed his right toe on the small hold he had been hanging from.

Roy wasn't thinking about what to do. His motions were reflex driven from years of climbing. Extending his right arm he reached the top edge of the overhang and pulled himself onto the ledge. Squatting on the ledge was a blond, blue eyed, muscular man. He smiled at Roy and stood with the grace of a seasoned climber unawed by the vertical exposure in front of him.

"Kurt Rail," he said and extended his hand. They shook hands.

"Roy Graham," Roy responded, "nice meeting you. I've got to bring Juan up now."

Roy quickly scanned the ledge for a crack large enough to hold a "friend." He found a crack, inserted the spring-loaded cam device and released the handle. Four heart-shaped discs with serrated edges rotated outward from the common axis and expanded inside the crack. The teeth of the discs bit into the granite holding the shaft of the "friend" like an anchor in the rock.

The "friend" was one of a number of innovative mountain climbing devices developed in the late seventies. They had become part of every climber's tool kit. Roy attached the hinged chain-link carabineer to the "friend" and tied a loop in his climbing rope using a figure-eight knot. He clipped the loop onto the carabineer anchoring him to the cliff. Sitting on a bench-sized rock that had broken from a ledge above; Roy wrapped the rope around his waist and pulled up the slack from the end of the rope that went to Juan.

"Juan, belay on. Come on up," Roy called down to Juan signaling that Juan could start climbing.

Roy pulled gently on the rope that disappeared over the edge with the thumb and index finger of his right hand like a fisherman testing a line for the slightest tug at bait. Roy could feel the slight changes in tension on the rope and the vibrations as Juan moved.

Juan started up the sheer face and climbed from one small handhold to another, jamming his toes into the crack until he was under the ceiling of the overhang. He placed his right hand in the small crack under the ceiling, and with his left hand removed the carabineer from the piton without removing it from the rope. The carabineer slid down the rope to his waist. Now there was nothing to keep him from falling except the rope going up to Roy.

"Okay, boss, watch me."

Roy's muscles instinctively responded, tightening slightly, ready to react if Juan should fall..

Juan shouted, "This doesn't look easy. I don't know how you did it."

He stretched out slowly and smoothly, still holding on with his right hand while reaching for the narrow lip of rock on the outer edge of the ceiling with his left hand. He touched the lip and started to curl his fingers on the rock to get a firm grip. The fingers of his right hand slipped out of the small crack he was using to hold onto the cliff. "Falling," he yelled, as he dropped from under the ceiling.

Roy's right arm quickly moved across his body to his left hip and gripped the rope tighter. The increase in friction of the rope around his waist stopped the rope.

Juan fell, then pendulumed out from the face and then back under the ceiling. When he finally stopped swinging, he glanced down 1,500 feet and closed his eyes. He tried to spit but his mouth was too dry.

"Hey, boss!"

"Okay, Juan," Roy yelled down to Juan, "feels like you came off. Make like James Bond and get out your fancy shoe lace."

Roy turned to Kurt, "You remember the scene in 'Never Say Never' when Roger Moore alias James Bond is climbing the rock face in Greece, and prussiks up the rope with his shoe lace while the bad guy on top is trying to knock the piton loose with his gun? I love the scene."

"Yeh," Kurt said, laughing lightly, "I like the spy stuff."

Juan took an ascender, a mechanical device that will slide up a rope but not down, from his harness and clipped it onto the rope above him. He slid the ascender up the rope and stood on a loop attached to it. He slid a small knot attached to his harness up the rope, released the pressure on the ascender, then sat in the harness.

Juan had moved up a foot and a half. He moved the ascender up the rope again, stood, then slid the small knot up the rope and sat down. He slowly climbed up the rope until he found a small ledge where he could get a handhold and footing. "Okay, boss, pull in the slack."

Roy pulled in the extra rope and Juan continued to climb. Juan reached the ledge and frowned in surprised to see a third person.

"Who's he?" Juan asked. "Where did he come from?"

Roy said, "Juan, meet Kurt. Kurt, meet Juan Martinez. He is my right arm most of the time and all of me when I'm out of town."

"Say, didn't I see you in a documentary four or five month ago?" Roy asked as he recognized Kurt. "Climbing the Dru. You were guiding a couple of German industrialists, East and West types, some form of unification symbol about working together to achieve a common goal."

"You have a good memory," Kurt said.

Roy smiled. "One doesn't have to have a good memory to remember the only significant climbing fcat in two years. By the way how did you get here?"

Kurt gestured upward with his thumb. My rope is around the corner and in a crack. You can't see it from here."

"Why you here?" Juan questioned skeptically.

"Mr. Graham," Kurt replied looking at Roy, "you are a hard person to catch up with and I wanted to meet you and find out if you need a climber or mountaineer for any of your upcoming trips."

"We still have to get to the top," Roy commented as he scanned the cliff in front of him for the sequence of handholds and footholds that he would use. "Let's talk at the top."

"Or on the way up," Kurt said. "Let's go." Kurt started up the sheer face parallel to where Roy planned to climb.

"Moves like a cat," Juan commented as he watched Kurt.

"Needs to, its a long way down. I'll go up and belay you. See you on top." Roy untied the figure eight he had used as an anchor when Juan was climbing. He ran the rope attached to his harness through the anchoring carabineer. As he climbed he would attach other anchors into small cracks and clip his rope to the anchor with a carabineer. In this way he could only fall as far as the distance to the last anchor.

Before Roy started up he tied a knot in a section of rope in front of Juan, anchoring Juan to the wall. Juan gave Roy a thumbs-up signal when he was ready to belay. "Okay, boss. Have a good trip."

Roy moved up the face with the grace of a ballet dancer. He thought about how different rock climbing was from hauling a sledge across a glacial field like a mule in front of a plow.

His movements brought him within talking distance of Kurt, as they both searched for small cracks or ledges for their fingers and bumps on the face for their rubber soled shoes. Roy said, hanging briefly with his right hand before chinning himself to where he could jam his left hand into a crack, "Come into my office. I'd offer you a chair but there aren't any. You will have to enjoy the scenery."

"Thanks," Kurt said. "I'll just take this big crack and make myself at home. As I indicated, I'm looking for some work in the area for the summer, if possible. I get around the world by working as a freelance guide." He searched for a handhold. "The pay isn't always good and the jobs are short but I do get to see the interesting places."

Roy was looking at a ledge just above his fingertips. "We don't have any trips scheduled at the moment, but I will keep you in mind. When we get to the cars I'll get your phone number so I can get in touch with you."

Roy lept up and grabbed the lip of a ledge with the fingers of his right hand. He placed a toe on the cliff and pushed enough to raise his left hand to the top. He pulled himself up to where he could see onto the ledge. "Ah, the top."

"Give me a minute," he yelled over to Kurt, "I'll bring Juan up and we can talk."

Kurt gestured in the direction behind Roy. "There is a quick way down the back side. I'll meet you at the cars." Kurt pulled up the rope he had used to rappel down to meet Roy, scrambled over a small pile of boulders and disappeared.

"Juan!" Roy shouted down the cliff. "Belay on."

Juan arrived on the top. "Where's Kurt's-his-face?"

"Whoa there, partner," Roy said noticing the dislike in Juan's voice. "He's okay. He just went down the backside. We'll meet him at the cars."

Roy and Juan set up their rappel and descended the backside to a series of ledges that led them to the base of the cliff. Kurt wasn't there but had left a card with a phone number on Roy's car.

Three days later Roy called Kurt and got an answering machine. "Kurt, this is Roy Graham. Something has come up that you might be interested in. Get back to me as soon as possible. It's kind of a crazy project with a tight timetable. So long."

Raymond Wallace, President of Wallace Images stood up at the end of a long glass conference table. The walls appeared to be opal grey glass and blank. "Let's get this meeting started. I'm concerned about our market position and why Krager Enterprises keeps beating us to the punch. If we are going to win in this market we have to have better marketing and better communications ...ah.. cooperation within this team. There is too much fighting between departments. We have to find a new way to work together."

Harry Kuznets, Director of Finance, leaned over to whisper to Grant Barnsworth, "Oh boy, here it comes, this year's trip."

"Harry, you have something to add?" Raymond glared at Harry.

Harry remained seated. "No, sir. Well, I was just thinking. We in Finance have been thinking a get-together would be useful so others could see people in Finance as being on the same team."

Grant Barnsworth spoke through clenched teeth, trying to keep his lips from moving, "Geeze, Harry, you'll need a lip condom if you keep this up."

"What does the Director of Information Systems think of Mr. Kuznet's idea?" Raymond Wallace said moving his stare from Harry to Grant.

Grant stood abruptly. "Sir, I think Harry has a good idea here. I know that the Information Systems Department seems to be perceived as having a glass wall around it and inaccessible to specialized work groups. A company picnic would be appropriate."

"Interesting," Raymond responded in a sarcastic tone. "You two are reading my thoughts, but with the same limitations you read the writing on the wall. I am not concerned with the rest of the people in your groups. I am concerned about those of you in this room, now"

"Each year we take an executive retreat with the idea of understanding one another a little better. Last year, St. Pete. What happened? Within a week everybody was back to the same bickering. The Aspen trip the year before. Same thing!"

"I want to do something different. This time no cushy bungalows where you sneak around, or bars where you get soused."

"Sir." Brad Longstretch interjected hesitantly, "these get- togethers reinforce the fabric of..."

Raymond cut him off. "I've had enough of this wimpy-touchy-feely stuff you guys in Human Resources come up with. Show me where happy means productive."

Brad's voice toughened, "Sir, the consensus in behavioral research is..."

Raymond cut him off again, "The only consensus we have is we are losing our technological edge. This group seems to lack that one singular focus we need to stay ahead. I thought our hike up Mt. Washington last spring would help you focus on the peak experience of reaching the summit together. All you did was complain about the blisters. So here is what we are going to do."

Tom Gilmore leaned over to Ralph Dresner, "Give you odds that here comes the announcement of this year's Lets Get Together In The Great Out-Of-Doors."

Ralph whispered back, "It's not always that bad."

"Oh!" Tom kept his eyes on Raymond Wallace while he responded to Ralph, "I don't think banging Todd's wife in the surf is what he meant by a peak outdoor experience."

"What are you talking about?" Ralph said, loud enough for several others to hear.

Tom scoffed, "Don't act surprised. I'll show you the pictures next time you make a run for my job."

Raymond hit his water glass with a pencil. "What the hell is the Research and Development

Department conferring about now? How to stick it to Engineering?"

"Not exactly," Tom responded.

"As I was starting to say," Raymond continued, "we are going to find a way of working and surviving together or this company is dead.

"Did any of you see the article in the paper last week about the fellow who just skied solo across Greenland to celebrate the centennial of Freidhoff Nansen's historic trip?" In case you did not see the article, his name is Roy Graham. He is going to be working with us. I have asked him to set up a challenge that you can't escape from. You are going to learn to work as a team to survive."

Harry Kuznets, looking across the table to Marcy Wallingford, who asked, "Who is Freidhof Nansen?"

Marcy Wallingford shook her head and asked of nobody in particular, "Why do we do this?"

Grant responded, "Our jobs."

Raymond glared at Grant, pushed the intercom button on his phone, and said, "Miss Peabody send in Mr. Graham."

The humming of motors running accompanied the dimming of lights. A three- dimensional holo-gram of a mountain range appeared over the con-ference table.

Roy Graham entered from Raymond Wallace's office where he had been watching the meeting. The wall of the office adjoining the conference room was a one-way mirror. Sound pick-ups allowed him to hear the conversations, even the whispers. While he listened and watched the meeting he reviewed the personnel files that Raymond Wallace had set out for him.

"Good morning," Roy Graham started talking without an introduction. "What we are going to do is fly to here." He. pointed with a red holographic, tent-shaped locator to a small flat section of a glacial valley. The head of the glacier was at the base of an enormous cliff topped by overhanging blocks of ice from another glacier that led to a rock summit. The sides of the valley surrounding the locator were steep and led to smaller summits. The entire display was of rocky peaks and flowing ice covered with rocks that had fallen from above.

The image was one very large glacial valley in the middle of the Fairweather range northwest of Juneau. It was surrounded by peaks. The locator was on a glacier that was a small tributary that flowed into a larger glacier. It in turn merged with other glaciers flowing to the ocean thirty miles to the south like a long tapestry made with threads of rock.

Zooming back from the valley, the cameras from the three satellites that were used to create the display revealed nothing but glaciers and peaks to the north and south. The Pacific Ocean was thirty miles to the west.

"From here we move 45 miles along this glacial system, then climb over this 10,000 foot ridge into this glacial system. From here we move across a fifteen-mile-wide glacier, cross the shoulder of Mt. La Perouse and descend to the South Lituya glacier. We follow that to Lituya bay.

"This is spectacular country. I spent two years up here with an exploration mining company. The glaciers are big, the cliffs are big and the challenges are big. You should find this an interesting trip. We should be gone fourteen to fifteen days, weather permitting."

"Mr. Wallace," Roy said as he handed him the pointer, "I'll let you discuss how we proceed."

Roy Graham left the quiet conference room through the door into Raymond Wallace's office. Everyone was still staring at the image in front of them when he opened up the viewing window.

Roy reopened the personnel files. He found it easier to remember the information when he could match the security photo in the file with the face of the person at the table and their posture and actions.

Jim Wallace, Vice President and younger brother of Raymond Wallace, stood and announced, "I've been quiet up till now but this is absurd. You can't expect us to take on such a ...a..."

Raymond countered, still seated, "Why, little brother, I've never heard you at such a loss for words. Maybe you are right. I've had such high expectations about the things I thought we all could do. Since we can't seem to do the everyday common things, maybe we should take on the preposterous." He stood and waited while Jim Wallace, his younger brother and Vice President, sat down.

"Damn right," the elder approved. It's time to find our limits."

Ralph Dresner murmured to himself, "He has got to be kidding."

Tom Gilmore said in an apparent attempt at humor, "There are no Macdonald's or Chez Roger's out there, and I don't think there will be pizza delivery. How will we eat?"

"Good question, Tom." Raymond explained, "Several strategic air drops will be used to provide basic provisions. At each drop we should be able to pick up three to four days of food and fuel. There will be no communications with the outside world· until we reach the coast."

He raised his right hand to block any more questions.

"Brad, I want you to give Mr. Graham a tour of the facilities and have him spend some time with each person here. He needs to find out what he has to deal with."

"Tom, stick around."

"Okay, meeting adjourned. We leave in two days."

Brad Longstreth shouted over the shuffling of papers and chairs, "Our families?" The room fell quiet.

Raymond responded, "Tell them whatever you tell them when you leave town for two weeks."

Everyone left as Tom Gilmore walked over to Raymond. Tom Gilmore and Raymond Wallace had been working together since Raymond started Wallace Images fifteen years before.

"Tom, this was a brilliant idea of yours. I didn't know you liked this outdoor stuff. I won't let on it was you who suggested the trip. The others might not appreciate your insight. How did you come up with it?"

Tom looked down modestly, "I had heard from an acquaintance about Roy Graham. Graham, it seems, comes up with some unique approaches to corporate problems. Apparently he has advanced degrees as well as corporate experience. He even worked in the White House on some organizational problems. I know we have been having some internal problems. He sounded like someone who might be able to help."

Roy heard a knock on the routine access door into the office. He slipped the personnel files back into Raymond Wallace's desk and closed the viewing panels. "Come in."

"I'm Brad Longstreth, Director of Human Resources." Brad walked across the office. The walls were lined with pictures of Raymond Wallace, various generals and admirals, and other military personnel in front of ships and aircraft. Brad extended his hand to Roy. They shook hands. Brad's hand seem white and soft against Roy's leathery, calloused hand that still had signs of being scraped hard against the granite cliff a few days before.

"I've been here ten years and have always been impressed with Mr. Wallace's offices. They have been like technology museums."

"There are other offices?" Roy asked.

"Oh, no, I was referring to the two other offices Mr. Wallace has had. Since I've been with Wallace Images there have been two major expansions. Six years ago we added a second building to support Research and Development. Then four years ago a third building was added. The three are separated by a triangle shaped courtyard. Each time there was an expansion Mr. Wallace changed his office. This one apparently has all the most recent communications and control systems built into it. None of the staff, including me, have been privy to what Mr. Wallace can do from here. It is almost like some of the new technology they develop here."

Brad led Roy down a windowed hall that overlooked a room where computer boards were being tested. The room was brightly lit. The workers wore face masks and green or white caps over their hair. "I saw some of the TV coverage of your Greenland trip.

Doesn't thirty-five days without someone else around get lonely?"

"Some think so," Roy answered absent-mindedly, studying the room below, "It's not as bad as spending thirty-five days with someone you don't like."

"I didn't know anything about this trip that Raymond called you here for," Brad commented as if trying to get Roy to explain more about the reason for the trip.

They had moved to another window overlooking a room in which the workers had white suits, caps and shoes and wore masks.

"This is the clean room where they assemble the chips that are the heart of our new 'Virtual Screen' display."

"What does it do?" Roy asked.

Brad explained. "It provides a flat-screen, three-dimensional image for computers. Sort like a credit card hologram that can be changed. Our R&D staff developed the original concept. The first models were made in Silicon Valley, in California. We just started our own assembly process this past year."

"I haven't seen them in the computer stores."

"You probably won't for a while," Brad explained, "the primary use is military. Data from three satellites is used to generate a three-dimensional landscape, I mean, image."

"Like the one in the conference room?"

"Sort of," Brad hesitated. "Actually not too many people have seen that, either. Most of the work is done in the R&D lab in the building across the courtyard. It is one of our new developments. That was only the second time I'd seen it. I'm surprised you were allowed to see it, use it. Do you have Top Secret clearance?"

"Something like that," Roy answered as he continued down the passage. They passed another window. Its surface was at an angle so they could see into a courtyard where staff could relax, eat lunch and get together. The first two stories of one of the walls across the three-walled courtyard appeared to be a large mural of the pyramids in Egypt.

"The walls in the courtyard contain large holographic displays," Brad said. "but they are only two-dimensional. Some are being installed in theatres. They can be used to provide scenes from anywhere in the world. Last week it was a Parthenon motif. Next week it is supposed to be a view of the moons of Mars from Mars. I guess I'll miss that one if I go on this trip of yours."

"What operation is that over there?" Through a window across the courtyard Roy could see Grant Barnsworth and Ian McGregor in an energetically gestured discussion.

"Oh, dear." Brad seemed embarrassed. "That is Grant's office. Information Systems. He has one of the newest of the large Cray super computers. It looks like he is having another argument with Ian. Ian thinks that the newer generation of networked desktop computers will be a better way for day-to-day operations to work together. It seems to be an argument that has gone on since Ian started here four years ago."

Brad hesitated.

Roy said, "Raymond wants me to understand this place. No secrets, Okay?"

Brad continued, "Ian wants to use some of the new ideas coming out of R&D for three dimensional modeling of the paper flow and work flow within Wallace Images to provide better management. He calls it Virtual Operations Simulation. They both get pretty heated up about it. Grant's general position is over-his-dead-body."

"Ian thinks better internal management with PC's could have prevented the budget problems in one of the communications projects." Brad stared at the two across the courtyard for a few seconds. "Sometimes I think Grant is too stubborn."

"If you are going to talk to people where do you want to start?" Brad gestured he wanted to continue down the hall.

Roy looked Brad in the face and smiled. "How about with you. Lets go to your office. Among other things, can you give me a staff roster and an overview of who does what?"

They took an elevator to the first floor and went to Brad's office. Brad pushed a couple of keys on his computer, A printed page slid onto his desk.

Roy studied the list and mentally compared it with the files he had reviewed in Raymond Wallace's office. "Where are the hot spots?" he asked.

"What do you mean?" Brad asks.

Roy explained. "Mr. Wallace has asked me to organize some form of outing experience where everybody has to work together. He provided some insight into organizational issues that concern him."

Executive Staff
Wallace Images

Raymond Wallace	- President (15 years)
Tom Gilmore	- Director of Research and Development (15 years)
Grant Barnsworth	- Director of Information Systems (15 years)
James Wallace	- Vice President (13 years)
Brad Longstreth	- Director Human Resources (10 years)
Harry Kuznets	- Director of Finance (8 years)
Michael Kirby	- Director of Engineering (7 years)
Todd Malcolm	- Director of marketing (6 years)
Ralph Dresner	- Assistant Director of Research and Development (6 years)
Ian McGregor	- Operations Manager (4 years)
Eugene Langley	- Chief Software Engineer (2 years)
Marcy Wallingford	- Chief Accountant (1 year)

Roy's tone changed to a quiet monotone. "What he has told me, and what you or anyone else tells me is basically confidential. I need to know your perceptions of the problems here at Wallace Images. You might see things differently than Mr. Wallace or the others. Also, keep in mind we will be taking a potentially hazardous trip and personal problems might have an impact on everyone."

"The scene we saw upstairs," Roy took a deep breath, "was that personal or a matter of professional differences?"

"It seems to be both." Brad shrugged his shoulders.

"How so?" Roy asked.

Brad looked past Roy, then back. "At times Grant seems to think that Ian is after his job. The thing is, Ian isn't interested in mainframe computers but networked desktop and laptop machines. He always says mainframes have their place and more attention should be given to providing better interfacing between the two systems. Grant then argues there are too many security problems if the two are connected."

Roy asked quickly, "What kind of security problems? Viruses? Proprietary data? Wallace Images designs? Espionage?"

Brad hesitated, stunned by the directness of Roy's questions. "Grant doesn't say specifically. However, there does seem to be a concern about leaks of design concepts but not from the computer departments. Rumors, if that. A feeling. Some people think that ideas are being stolen. On the other hand everybody knows it is a competitive business and lots of companies are working on concepts similar to what we are."

"Who is most vocal about the idea stealing?" Roy softened his voice.

Brad hesitated. "Tom Gilmore, the head of R&D, seems to point a finger at Ralph Dresner, his assistant, the assistant head of R&D. He thinks that Ralph has too many friends on the outside that are working for competitors. Ralph started working here about six years ago. That was about the same time we started to have problems."

"Who hired Ralph?" Roy asked. "Tom?"

"No," Brad said, "James Wallace hired him. There was a major proposal being developed for the Air Force and Ralph apparently had the right credentials. Tom started to complain about him early on. Tom said Ralph asked too many questions."

"Who else is rumored to be linked to ... stealing?" Roy asked, "if that is the concern."

"A couple of people suggest its James Wallace. He would like to see his brother fail so he could take over."

"We will talk some more later," Roy interrupted. "I should really spend a few minutes with the others. Can you introduce me to Harry Kuznets? I'll have lunch with James Wallace later."

Brad called Harry Kuznets's secretary and let her know Roy was coming.

"Harry is expecting you. His office is down the hall. You can't miss it. There is something I have to do or I'd take you there."

Harry Kuznets, Director of Finance, met Roy halfway across the office. "I get the impression Mr. Wallace, that is, Raymond, has given you the idea that this place is coming apart. I don't know what all the fuss is about. If James would make up his mind there wouldn't be so much rancor. R&D wants to spend a fortune exploring new ideas. My job as Director of Finance is to make sure they don't spend money on things that are not necessary for our mission. It's James; Mr. Wallace's brother's job to set the spending limits and decide what ideas we pursue. He is, after all, Vice President and has overall responsibility for the various projects. Every time I do my job, Tom Gilmore in R&D and Michael Kirby in Engineering jump on me like I'm the one sabotaging the future of the company."

"After they dump on me, they blame marketing for cutting off their projects and they blame marketing for not promoting the projects to justify their need to spend. I think they are driving poor Todd over the edge. He already has an alcohol problem and they just make it worse."

Roy thanked Harry Kuznets for his time and insight and left.

"How did your presentation go?" Juan asked when Roy returned. Roy and Juan used a renovated fire station on Capital Hill for their warehouse and office and Roy used the upstairs for his living quarters. Juan was sorting rock climbing equipment into small piles.

How many people do I have to provide gear for?"

"Plan on twelve people, Kurt, you and me. It is a crazy group," Roy answered. "High tech stuff. They have been around for fifteen years. Started to grow about six to seven years ago and started having lots of problems. Everybody blames somebody else for the problems they are having. I think it is just growing pains."

"I briefed them on the trip. I don't think they really know what they are getting into. So far their outdoor trips have involved staying in ski lodges or Hawaiian wicki-wickis and having seminars after dinner drinks. This is going to involve two weeks of backpacking, climbing and sleeping on glaciers."

"Have you heard from Kurt? How about the permits to land in Canada and traverse into the U.S.? Anything from George Baker in Juneau? Of all the bush pilots up there he is the best. He will take us by floatplane to Lituya Bay. From there two choppers to get us to base camp on the Canadian side of the Brady Glacier. We have to try to get everyone out there at about the same time if possible. Hard to say what they would do to each other if we left them alone. He can use float planes to pick us up in Lituya Bay on our way back."

"Bad bunch?" Juan asked.

"Not really," Roy answered while he spread out a map of the area where they would be traveling. "There is a lot of insecurity and something going on I can't put my finger on. There are the usual organizational battles. The more I talked to people the worse it got. Once we have them on the ice they can't run away. Maybe they will start to talk to one other. Past experience with group encounters and "T" groups and those touchy-feely programs, as Raymond Wallace calls them, doesn't exactly turn me on. My hope is that when they really have to depend on each other to get out of a crevasse or up a cliff they will learn to communicate."

"Sounds like the drug abuse crowd we had a couple of years ago," Juan said.

"Might be, at least one person has a drinking problem. There weren't any suggestions about drugs but keep your eyes open. You might want to bring your referee's whistle and striped shirt. Some of these folks really don't get along. I'll let you figure out who doesn't like who and quiz you at the end of the trip."

"Thanks a lot, boss." Juan laughed then frowned. "By the way, Kurt called. Wouldn't talk to me but said you can get him. The number is on your desk. Also, I've made arrangements with the manager at the local REI store for us to come in after hours. A couple of their staff will help get everyone fitted with parkas, sleeping bags and clothing. They already have our list for tents, ice axes, stoves and other gear. I faxed the three air drop locations to George Baker in Juneau. He didn't think he would have any problems. Are you sure you don't want a radio in the base camp equipment?"

"You have been busy," Roy said. "No radio. This group has to know they are isolated. If necessary I'll trek to the first air drop and get the radio. That should be only two days without communication at most. We will have a location transponder with us. That's strictly between you and me. General Langston will be able to track our progress. I can modulate the signal with aluminum foil if need be."

Juan questioned, "Why is the General involved?"

"He is an old friend who sometimes uses me as a guinea pig, so I told him he owed me one. Strictly an emergency backup."

"Boss, sometimes I get the feeling you don't tell me everything."

"Juan," Roy joked, "did you tell your wife everything?"

"No, and look what happened!"

"Touché. There are some things going on that I haven't figured out yet."

CHAPTER 2
GLACIERS

The two engines generated a vibration that started at the front of the plane and worked its way back past the eight passengers to the tail, and then returned to the front. Roy Graham, Marcy Wallingford, Tom Gilmore, Raymond Wallace, Grant Barnsworth, Brad Longstreth and Michael Kirby watched the coastline pass under them. To the left were the blue waters of the Pacific spotted with white-capped waves. Small fishing boats could be seen hanging onto the mile-long fishing nets that acted like sea anchors. The boats and nets looked like streaks of grey paint on the blue and white canvas. To the right was an endless row of mountains and high ridges separated by white and brown ribbons of glaciers covered with rocks. Large glaciers half-a-mile or more wide flowed from the mountains down to the ocean, pushing their snouts into the currents. Grey-silted glacier water flowed into the Pacific and turned south as it mixed with the currents running past the glaciers. When the plane passed over a glacier it would drop several feet. George Baker, the pilot, explained that the glacier cooled the air so they lost the lift associated with the warmer air over the land. When they finished crossing the glacier the plane rose rapidly. He said there were times in the fog that he knew where he was by how far the plane dropped and how long it took to fly over the glacier.

Grant asked Roy, "Are glaciers just rivers of ice?"

Roy responded, "They are similar to the extent they are frozen water and flow downhill under the influence of gravity."

George Baker, watching the horizon shouted over the engine noise, "Most of the bays, inlets and lakes in Southeastern Alaska are the result of glacial action. Glaciers got started during the ice ages, when there was so much snow in the winter that it could not melt during the summer and the amount was sufficient for a large buildup of accumulated snow. During the cold periods of the "Ice Age" the snow accumulations were thousands of feet deep. When the buildup gets high enough the pressure of the weight of snow and ice causes the ice at the bottom to become plastic and flow. It flows into cracks and weak rock and digs down to the hard bedrock. Glaciers are nature's version of a giant bulldozer which scrapes away the rock underneath to great depths."

Grant said, "It looks like some of the glaciers are going north and south instead of down the mountain."

"Most of the glaciers running north and south are following old earthquake fault lines. The east and west running glaciers are due to the land rising and the ice keeping pace. There are lots of earth-quakes and fault lines up here."

"Why do they follow fault lines?" someone asked.

"The bedrock along the fault lines has been cracked and weakened. The glacier can dig in along the weak rock. Path of least resistance."

Grant asked, "Why is that river white?" as he pointed to a stream they were passing over.

Roy answered, "As a glacier flows downhill it drags along the rocks it has surrounded and pushes them along the top of the bedrock. The pressure of rocks grinding over bedrock century after century turns them into a fine flour-like powder and pol-ishes the bedrock. Glacier water runoff carries the rock flour into the rivers below."

The pilot rolled the plane so the passengers on the left could look down at the coastline. Water from a river carrying rock-flour was milky white and sent a cloudy streamer into the ocean. The streamer flowed out several hundred yards before turning south as it mixed with the offshore current. He rolled the plane to the right so the other passengers could watch the remains of former mountains wash-ing into the ocean.

Roy continued the explanation. "When the Ice Age ended and the glaciers started melting, the bed-rock that was not worn away, rose as peaks above the receding glacial surface. All the valleys and lakes in southeastern Alaska are the result of glacial fin-gers digging into and gouging out the bedrock. The large glaciers like the Malspena and the Brady are the accumulation of ice from hundreds of smaller glaciers now fed by winter snows and the slow rising of the mountains along the Pacific under the thrust of tectonic plate movement. When the spring and summer melt is greater than the autumn and winter snowfall the glacier stagnates. The pressure to move the ice downhill lessens and the glacier recedes. In some places there isn't enough new ice to push the glacial flow over a rock barrier and the melting ice forms a lake."

"The larger glaciers flow to the ocean and some places are so covered with dirt that forests grow on top of them. The trees eventually fall into the ocean when the glacier is eroded by wave action."

The pilot announced that they were passing over Lake Crillon and could see Lituya Bay a few miles ahead.

Lituya bay is a six-mile body of water shaped like a fat "T." The top of the "T" runs north and south and was formed by the south-flowing Lituya glacier turning westward where it merged with the north-flowing Crillon glacier, then flowing west to the ocean. The ocean flooded the valley left by the receding of the single glacier and the two that fed it. The bay is pear-shaped with the narrow stem reaching into the Pacific Ocean. The opening to the bay from the ocean is wide enough for fishing boats to pass.

A forest of one-hundred-foot-high Sitka spruce grows along the ocean shore on both sides of the opening to the bay. Near the middle of the bay are the remains of the top of a small mountain called Cenotaph Island. The head end of the bay is a mountain that rises steeply to five thousand feet. The two glaciers that formed the bay still flow along the base of the mountain and push large blocks of ice into the bay.

The pilot continued his descriptions. "A number of fishermen are superstitious about Lituya Bay. Some would go into the bay to get ice from the small icebergs for their holds in order to keep their catch of fish cold. Others would not take their boats into the bay, either fearful of the icebergs or the stories they had heard about mystery waves that would swamp boats. The tree line on Cenotaph Island indicates at least two instances where waves have washed the trees away, one to an altitude of thirty feet and another over fifty feet.

He flew inland. "Below us is Lake Crillon," he said and made a sharp banking turn that caused a few groans, in order to circle over the lake. "Lake Crillon, like many of the mountain lakes, has been formed by the receding of a deep glacier. As the forward motion of the glacier stops because of general warming in the climate, the front end melts. The water is trapped behind the rock barrier that the glacier had not yet scoured away. If the water could escape the remains of the glacier would be a boulder-filled valley.

"Over several centuries the Crillon glacier receded leaving a deep lake several miles long and half-a-mile wide. It will grow longer as the Crillon glacier recedes. The glacier still dominates the eastern end of the lake. Blocks of glacier ice the size of large houses would calve off the front and drift in the quiet lake.

"The tip of an iceberg in the lake might be no bigger than a large car or truck but ninety percent of it was under water. Rain and sun erode the top and waves lapping at the floating mass of ice wash away the edge of the top forming a large flat shelf a foot below the surface. The submerged shelf can reach out fifteen to twenty-five feet from the ice exposed above the surface.

"The icebergs develop a delicate floating balance. If the balance was upset due to erosion or a piece breaking off, the iceberg goes into a slow-motion roll. It could turnover if even a few large chunks were removed from the tip."

"A number of fishermen, out to get ice cubes for their evening drink, have found their boats lifted by the submarine shelf that rose when the iceberg balance was upset after they knocked off a piece of ice with an axe or shot off a piece with a pistol or rifle, and the iceberg turned over. At times the weight of the long shelf rising in the air as the iceberg rotated would split the iceberg and the two parts would sink and rise in a slow dance. Rings of small waves would radiate out from the two. As they oscillated up and down they bumped, breaking small chunks of ice and filling the area with white debris."

Roy added to George's discussion, "The ice in Lake Crillon has had an alluring property for hunters and fisherman who have camped there. The ice sings."

Marcy asked, "Like mermaids calling to lonely sailors?"

"Why not?" Roy answered, "The ice that has been formed under tremendous pressure for centuries is crystal clear. When the ice is placed in a drink it melts and the pressure inside is released like a coiled spring. The outer shell of the ice cracks slightly before it melts and the cracking causes the ice to "ring" like a brandy snifter being struck with a fingernail."

George dropped the plane below the tree line and flew above the lake to give everyone a close view. He said, "One small advertising firm in New York imports the lake ice for a novelty at extravagant parties. The problem was, most of the time at the parties there was so much noise that the guests could not hear the sound in their drinks. Those who carried their drinks with them when they slipped away for a quiet romantic moment have often been surprised to hear the singing ice."

Raymond said, "We'll get some when we go back."

George gained altitude, climbing over the trees at the western end of the lake and over a ridge that separated Lake Crillon from the South Crillon Glacier and flew over Lituya bay.

A few minutes later he pointed down and indicated they would be landing. He took the plane down to two hundred feet and circled over the bay to find a clear landing path through the maze of icebergs.

"My God," Brad exclaimed, "if we get any closer to those trees we'll crash."

Finishing the circle, George took the plane out over the ocean, turned and came in low over the forest of hundred-foot spruce trees guarding both sides of the entrance to the bay. He dropped abruptly to a few feet above the water, leveled out and then let the plane glide down slowly. As the pontoons skimmed the surface he revved the engine to a roar to compensate for the drag of the water. Under control, he settled the plane on the surface and idled the engines. He taxied around a number of icebergs and drifted up to a log- strewn beach at the mouth of Coal Creek.

The passengers got out and walked a pontoon to where they could jump onto the beach. The pilot handed Roy, standing on a pontoon, packs and bags and a few boxes. Roy in turn passed them to those on the beach. When the plane was cleared of gear the pilot indicated he would be back in a couple of hours with the others and that the choppers would follow. Before he started the engines the only sound was a few sea gulls and the hushed roar of several waterfalls at the head end of the bay.

"It is so quiet I can hear my heart beating," Marcy said in a whisper just as the engines roared into action.

George revved the engines sending water and wind onto those standing on the edge of the beach. The plane taxied into the bay, around some large chunks of ice and turned west. The pitch of the engine increased and the plane moved forward, picking up speed.

The pontoons lifted out of the water, leveled out and skimmed along the surface. Seagulls scattered. The sound echoed back and forth across the bay and amplified in intensity. The plane continued down the bay a distance before lifting off the water. It banked left and disappeared from sight behind the forest lining the bay and with it the sound of the engine diminished. Shortly the only sounds that could be heard were the cries of the gulls as they settled back to the water's surface.

"I've never been anyplace so quiet," Marcy said.

"Kind of chilly out here," Brad said, flapping his arms across his chest.

Roy said, "Pick up some sticks and we'll start a fire."

Brad, Marcy and Raymond started to gather twigs, branches and dry moss and lichen from the edge of the forest twenty feet from the water.

"What a waste of time," Michael Kirby said, "We could be testing..."

Raymond, returning with an armload of fire material cut him off. "Stow it Kirby. There is a reason we are out here. If you want to test something, test your Boy Scout skills and start a fire."

Tom and Grant found a log to sit on. Tom set up a chess set he had pulled from his pack.

Raymond explained to Roy that Tom's passion was chess and that he carried his board with him everywhere.

Michael started some moss and small twigs burning and piled large pieces of pitch-laden branches on top. The smoke from the fire rose straight up.

"I knew you could do it if you set your mind to it," Raymond said to Michael.

Marcy started to walk down the rocky beach towards the ocean and returned. "The mosquitoes are eating me alive," She said.

Roy opened a pack and pulled out three bottles of insect repellant and passed them around. The pungent aroma filled the air as everyone rubbed the liquid onto their faces, necks and hands.

In air was cool and crisp. Roy suggested they put on their down parkas to stay warm because they were going to be sitting while waiting for the others.

Marcy put on her red parka and gloves for protection from the mosquitoes and returned to her walk down the beach. Brad and Michael stood by the fire and took turns putting dried branches on it. From time to time they moved away from the smoke as a gentle breeze shifted its direction.

Raymond and Roy walked up the beach to a moss-covered log where they sat. They could see the campsite and Marcy farther down the beach but were far enough away that nobody could hear them talking.

"How did Wallace Images get started?" Roy asked.

"I was in the Air Force for twenty years as a contracting officer," Raymond Wallace answered. "Originally I had a degree in electrical engineering. I tried to keep abreast of the developing computer and graphics display technologies. I knew that when I retired I wanted to start a small company. The technology fascinated me then and still does."

"I was also fascinated with the organizational aspect of making technology work. For a couple of years before I retired I tried to identify some bright engineers and programmers who had an inclination for innovation that I might recruit. When I did retire I stayed in touch with some friends at the Department of Defense and some of the contractors I'd met over the years.

"I was able to get some contracts with companies to do design work and to develop prototypes in such a way as to avoid conflicts of interest and provisions that I not work on projects that I was involved in at DOD for at least two years."

"One of the people I had met earlier was Tom Gilmore. He was, and still is a brilliant techie. Kind of a loner. I could suggest a few things to him and he would come back with a few questions, disappear into his lab and come out in a couple of days with a working prototype. I would go out and peddle it. We worked like that for years. We were close. It was kind of like our minds met on the techie fringe."

"We didn't have to deal with production because somebody else always built the final products from prototypes that Tom developed. Tom didn't want to deal with the problems of production. The only thing he has liked about production once we started, was what he called the endless supply of parts. He really screwed up production a couple of times by pilfering production inventory for use in the R&D labs. Kirby, in production, even had to go down to Radio Shack to get parts to keep the assembly line going. We nearly had a blood bath on that one," Raymond chuckled. "There have been some moments. Anyway, Tom was happy creating."

"The only other thing that he seems to do is play chess. Always has. Every year he would go to a chess tournament or two. He is good. He even had a draw against Gasperoff."

"How about Grant Barnsworth? Didn't he start with you and Tom?" Roy asked.

"Pretty much from day one," Raymond answered. "When I was starting I knew we needed some computer support for design work and simulation of prototypes in a working environment. A friend at Wright-Patterson Air Force base suggested I contact Grant. He was working in a small company that had a contract with Wright-Patt and didn't seem happy with the company he was with. They were milking his ideas and not giving him any credit. He jumped their ship and has never looked back."

"In the last few years, though, he seems to have lost some of his original zeal. His computers have gotten bigger and faster and more expensive. His commitment to security seems to bog him down. I am not sure he is able to stay flexible and stay on top of the broader range of computer technology that has been evolving."

"Early on, maybe twelve years ago, Grant added a simple accounting program to the system. It was abandoned because of a conflict that occurred that interrupted design work. Tom Gilmore had lost some critical design work. The furor that occurred resulted in a general dictum that no business oriented work was to be placed on the design machine platforms. Administrative work would be done by hand and project tracking would be done by hand."

"I suggested once that a PC could be used for project management. Grant was generally unresponsive to this suggestion and even stonewalled the incursion of PC's. While I have dropped all conversations with Grant about PC's, one of the things I hope to work out over the next two weeks is his relationship with Ian."

Roy interrupted, "What do you mean?"

Raymond answered, "I sort of suggested to little brother James that we needed some PC support and left Ian's resume' lying on my desk. He hired Ian and lets everyone know it was his idea. That is exactly what I wanted. I don't want Grant thinking I am the one stabbing him in the back as he calls it. You might have gathered already he doesn't like Ian's approach to computer usage and gets paranoid about operational data. Last year Grant even removed a number of accounting functions from his department that were on a non-design-support partition of his AS-400 and farmed them out to an accounting service so that Ian couldn't integrate those accounting functions into some of his efforts. Kind of cutting off his nose to spite his face. I really think it is better if he thinks James is responsible."

"Speaking of James," Roy asked, "When did he join Wallace Images?"

"In our third year. That was twelve years ago," Raymond answered. "James graduated from the University of Washington with a double major in electrical engineering and business administration. I had promised our mother that I would look out for him. So, when he graduated we hired him."

Roy and Raymond talked for nearly two hours before the plane returned with the rest of the team. Roy felt he had a better sense of the history of Wallace Images but still did not have grasp of the problems. He knew that he had to listen to the others. Even Raymond's perceptions might be clouded.

Gulls screamed in protest and circled high above the bay as the plane taxied into the shore. When the propeller stopped spinning, the rest of the team scrambled to the beach.

"Wow," Todd Malcom exclaimed, "did you ever see so much ice?"

There was a short flurry of comparisons of what each had seen on the flight.

George Baker unloaded their equipment, handing it to Roy who stood on a pontoon. Roy passed each item to Michael who was standing at the edge of the water. Michael, in turn, passed the items on to whoever came over to receive it. Marcy held the line tied to the pontoon to keep the plane from drifting. Before George Baker took off the second time he handed Roy a salmon and suggested there would be enough time to cook it before the helicopters arrived.

When the sound of the plane's engine disappeared and the screaming of the agitated gulls returned, Marcy handed Harry Kuznets some insect repellant. "Here, boss, you might need this."

Juan went into woods and returned with a thick huckleberry branch that had three forks on it. He split each branch and fanned them out so there were six radiating spokes. Roy had sliced the length of the inside of the salmon along both sides of the backbone and laid the two halves of it out flat. Juan supported the salmon by alternating the spokes of the branch between the flesh and skin side of the salmon so it looked like it was part of a fan. One spoke on the backside, the second, fourth and sixth spokes on the inside, the third and fifth spokes on backside. He stuck the base of the branch into the beach next to the hot coals of the fire.

The skin side of the flattened salmon beaded with oil as it cooked from the radiating heat of the coals. The oil dropped into the sand and smoldered filling the air with the smell of cooking fish. Half an hour later the salmon had been cooked and devoured. The sea gulls fought over the scraps of skin and bone that were thrown into the bay.

"Those gulls sound like a board meeting," Ian said, and shrugged his shoulders when nobody responded.

Todd asked, "What is that sound?"

A distant thumping punctuated with the cries of the circling gulls. The sound of three helicopters became distinct. Everybody was looking down the bay toward the ocean.

Ian pointed up and said, "There they are, up there."

Three helicopters circled high above the spire of smoke from the fire, then went north out over the bay and descended. They landed on the water riding on pontoons, a short distance up the bay then drifting into the beach.

The group's equipment was loaded inside and onto racks on the outside of the helicopters. The fire was doused with water. Everybody climbed into the helicopters to ride up to their first base camp area. Lituya Bay grew smaller and disappeared from view as they went around the southern shoulder of the mountain at the head-end of the bay.

As they moved east, all that was visible as far as anyone could see were brown and rust- colored rock peaks and ridges, snow slopes and glaciers. They passed the mountains that ran along the ocean and flew across what seemed an endless expanse of white snow and deep-shadowed crevasses.

"How big is this glacier?" Tom Gilmore asked. The pilot indicated it was thirty miles across in the direction they were moving.

The helicopters descended into the glacial valley from the north heading toward an 8,000- foot cliff. The west and east sides of the valley were bounded by ridges three to six thousand feet above the valley floor.

The north side opened onto a glacier that flowed to the west. From their position high above the glacier had the appearance of a woven Indian rug with symmetric black and brown patterns running its length and width. As they descended, the fabric of the glacial tapestry turned into piles of rock. Dirt and boulders that had rolled and crashed down the sides of the ridges moved on the top of the rivers of ice. As the ice from the glacier on which the rocks landed merged with another westward-moving gla-cier, the rocks from the two glaciers flowed together and formed a band of rock a hundred yards wide. Where two glaciers merged another ribbon of rock was added. It was hard to imagine that these patterns were only a slow-moving rock conveyor belt carrying mountains to the ocean. Maybe in a million years these rocks would be sand on the western rim of the Pacific Ocean.

The pilots turned the engines off and let the long blades slow down while the passengers disembarked. Packs, tents and climbing gear were unloaded and placed in piles thirty feet away. Everybody made three to four trips between the helicopters and the piles of equipment. After ten minutes the pilots restarted on the engines and the large blades quickly turned into a circular blur. One helicopter lifted up slowly then moved toward the glacier to the north, nose tilted down as if it were sniffing out the trail away from the valley. It cruised fifteen to twenty feet off the glacial floor for several hundred yards before climbing and disappearing to the west around the shoulder of the snow and rock ridge. The second helicopter rose, sniffed its way down the glacier, climbed and disappeared. The third followed the pattern.

No one spoke for several minutes. The sound of the helicopters echoed in their memories briefly and all was quiet. Everybody was looking to where the helicopters had disappeared. On the bay there had been the cries of the gulls and the breeze blowing through the trees. Here there was no sound.

Slowly all eyes started scanning the ridges, the avalanche paths of rock and ice that descended to the glacial floor and to the immense wall of rock to the south. A sudden explosion followed by the clattering sounds of tons of ice and rock cascading down from eight thousand feet above them filled the valley with a deafening roar. Everyone moved closer together involuntarily. Which way to run?

Roy said, "Look up there." He pointed at a forty-five to fifty-degree angle toward the cliff to the south.

Ice blocks the size of houses were pouring down like a waterfall, cascading off ledges, and breaking into smaller blocks.

Marcy asked, "Shouldn't we run?"

Roy chuckled, "Don't worry, it's over a mile away."

The waterfall like mass of debris slowly quieted down to a grey trickle of ice and rock. A cool movement of air swept by. Another two minutes went by in quiet.

Brad Longstreth whispered, "God it's quiet out here."

"And cold," Ralph added.

The sun was still high but the ridge to the west cast a shadow that filled the valley. The temperature was a little above freezing. The sun shining on the eastern ridge above the valley warmed the boulders that were held by the ice. A sun-warmed rock would occasionally slip from its icy grip and accelerate down the steep slope. A depression in the surface pitched the rock into space. When it struck the slope below it would knock blocks of ice and other rocks loose. Within seconds a thundering avalanche would be cascading into the valley.

Roy called to get the attention of the group. "Okay, everybody, Juan here, whom you met the other night is the mastermind behind the equipment. Not all of you have met Kurt Rail. He is one of the top mountaineers in the world and an expert on glacier travel. He has teamed up with us for this little adventure."

One by one everyone walked over and shook hands with Kurt. Their next action was to stamp firmly on the snow covering the ice to warm their feet.

Roy said, "For all practical purposes the sun has set but it won't get dark for several more hours. Last week was the first day of summer. While we are not as far north as the Arctic Circle it will stay light until 11:30 PM or so. Let's set up tents, heat up some water for coffee and make dinner. There will be two to a tent. Your first decisions of the trip will be to decide on your tent mate. Other decisions will be who cooks, who washes dishes, and were do we go to the bathroom."

Marcy, looking around at the open terrain and then at Roy asked,

"What about me?"

"Did you want to choose first?"

"No, where do I go? You know, to the bathroom."

Juan interjected, "Same place as everyone else."

"Juan thinks of everything," Roy said holding up a toilet seat attached to two poles. "Porta Potty. Everybody will get a turn at latrine duty. Juan will set it up the first night; so everyone pay attention. While there won't be a quiz, your understanding of the process will be evident to all. Also, we don't have an outhouse wall or modesty skirt so please, no snowballs while someone is using the facility. Juan, can you show us all how it works?"

Juan said, "Follow me." He walked up a slight slope and over the crown to a place just out of view of the campsite. First he stomped his boots down compacting the snow over an area three feet by two feet. He set the toilet seat and the poles on the compacted area. The poles went out to the edges of the prepared surface. He marked the location of the seat on the surface, then removed the seat and poles.

"When you dig the hole that will be under the seat, keep it as small and deep as possible." He then put the poles and seat on the surface over the hole he had dug to demoonstrate.

"How do we sit on that?" Marcy asked. "It's flat on the snow."

"No problem," Juan said. He then dug a small trench up to a foot in front of the toilet seat and then tapered the trench to within six inches of the seat. "Notice I've left about a foot of snow in front of the seat. Guys, you had better pee standing with the toilet seat up. Aim for the back of the wall. If you don't, the warm water will melt the front of the toilet system and you will have a big mess. Actually, you can stand over there about ten feet away for peeing. Just sit when you have to. When you are finished put the lid down. If it snows and freezes, I don't want to sit on an icy toilet seat."

As they returned to the campsite Marcy said to the sky, "I wonder if I can hold it for two weeks."

Grant offered, "It might not help your disposition."

James Wallace requested "Roy, could you make the tent assignments."

Raymond Wallace stared at his younger brother and shook his head and muttered, "You can't even make that simple a decision."

Brad Longstreth piped in, "I second that."

Roy asked, "Any objections to deferring your first decision?"

There was a short chorus of "No" and "That's okay."

Roy said, "Over the course of the trip we will change the arrangements. The primary consideration will be non-snorers will not be forced into a snorer's tent."

"Boss," Juan commented, "they are not laughing. They must be hungry."

"Okay. We anticipated this," Roy said as he pulled a slip of paper from his pocket and read off the list:

Mike	- James
Ian	- Ralph
Brad	- Grant
Marcy	- Kurt
Raymond	- Eugene
Todd	- Harry
Tom	- Juan
Me"	

"Since there are fifteen of us there will usually be one odd person in a tent by himself. Tonight it will be me."

"If the weather is really nice you might want to sleep outside the tent. The stars are spectacular when they finally come out. Some nights the Aurora Borealis is unbelievable."

Brad interrupted, "The what?"

"Northern Lights," Roy answered and continued his instructions for the evening. "Set your tents fifteen feet or so apart. Face the openings of the tents toward the glacier to the north, over there." Roy directed their attention to what appeared to be a landscape of boulders and ice. "Otherwise the draft coming down the big face will blow in the front door. Place the ground cloth inside the tents and your foam rubber pads on the ground cloth. The ground cloth will keep you dry as the ice under the tent melts. Also, in the unlikely event it rains, the ground cloth inside the tent won't collect water as it runs down the side of the tent."

Each tent pair carried their packs a few feet away from the central pile of equipment. There was a flurry of activity as tents were pulled from their bags and poles and stakes were sorted out. A couple of people read instructions and a few others figured out what had to be done.

The four tent poles consisted of seven sections, each held together with elastic cord. By holding one of the end sections and letting go of the others they would all spring into place and form one long pole. The poles were slid through loops along the seams up one side of the tent over the top and down the other side. The ends of the poles fitted into hooks and to the bottom of the corners of the hexagonal-shaped tent floor. From time to time someone would say, "Not that loop, the one next to it."

Raymond and Eugene shouted in unison, "TAH-DAH!" when they finished the first standing tent.

"Time to start dinner. Ralph, Todd, Mike, will you help Juan with the stoves. Kurt and I are going to scout the area to set up tomorrow's training sessions. The rest of you help set up the tents."

"Kurt, let's go find a snow slope steep enough to practice the self-arrest and a small crevasse that we can use for crevasse rescue." They threw ropes over their shoulders, picked up their ice axes and trudged off toward the west ridge.

Kurt indicated he had spotted some candidate sites about a quarter to a half-mile to the west. They did not bother to rope up. The crevasses were small and the glacier flow too rapid for the formation of hidden crevasses. The snow on the surface had already cooled down from the afternoon sun and was firm under foot. It made a crunching sound when they kicked their boots into the slope.

"Roy, why did you pick this part of the world?"

"Wanted to isolate the group as far from civilization as possible where everything they have to do is different from regular day-to-day living. I was familiar with this area since I had spent a total of ten months wandering around up here when I was in college. I worked for an exploration mining company. For two summers we had a base camp about twenty miles from here, across the glacier."

"Okay, here is what we want. That slope will be good for self-arrest and belay practice. That steep section to the right will work for simulated glacier rescue practice."

They stood in front of a sloped terrace that looked like the up-ramp in a multi-story parking lot. The bottom portion had a gentle slope off the front side. The higher up the ramp went the steeper the drop from the edge became. When the ramp was twenty feet above the bottom section where they stood the drop was vertical.

"We can have them climb that vertical face as if it were one side of a crevasse they had fallen into."

Kurt nodded, "Looks like it should work. What's our plan for the next couple of days?"

"We will spend three days here getting used to sleeping on the ice, learning self-arrest and crevasse extraction techniques and learning how to travel on a glacier. It will give them time to get used to walking with crampons on their feet and carrying forty and fifty- pound packs. Try to get them in a little better physical shape. Not all of them went to camp as kids. A few of them are not in very good shape. Raymond and Eugene are in excellent condition. James, Tom and Todd are in pretty poor condition. The rest are so- so to good. We have time to set a pace that everyone can handle and we will just take our time on the steep stuff on the other side of the glacier."

"It didn't look like we had enough supplies in camp for the trip," Kurt observed.

Roy explained, "There have been two supply drops between here and Mt. La Perouse over there, to the west. We will go over the pass on the north side of La Perouse and drop down to the Lituya glacier system. We should find another supply drop on the South Lituya glacier. We'll follow the South Lituya glacier down to Lituya Bay and signal Alaska Coastal Airlines for a pickup. There is a supply drop and a radio at the head end of the bay."

Kurt sniffed the air. "I think I can smell dinner cooking and its half a mile away."

"Race you to camp," Roy challenged.

Juan and the others looked up as Roy and Kurt charged down the hill. The snow flew away from their feet as they made long, almost jumping, strides down the slope. Titanium carabiners and aluminum ice pitons attached to their packs banged against each other.

"Hey, boss," Juan said. "I thought you said no man could beat you in a race to food on a glacier."

"That is right, my friend. This entity standing next to me is a spirit. He is not a man but the spirit of the glacier, born of the union of the god of the north and a beautiful Indian princess who wandered this glacier. Besides, he is hungrier than I am and hungry spirits travel faster than mortals. What's for dinner?"

Juan said, "Todd is the chef tonight. Ask him."

"Beef Stroganoff and apple pie. Do you realize that this is the first time I've ever cooked over a camp stove?"

A general groan emerged from the group.

"Smells good," Kurt offered.

Juan had dug a small trench that Todd could stand in so the surface of the glacier was waist high. A foot below the top he dug a shelf. Flat rocks were placed on the shelf and four single burner white gas stoves placed on the rocks and were purring busily. The snow from the pit was piled on the glacier behind the stoves to form a windbreak that kept the wind from blowing out the flames. Two large pots were bubbling with rehydrated beef stroganoff. Water was simmering in the other two. Several people were munching on Triscuits and cheese. Others were stirring powdered coffee or hot chocolate in their metal cups with metal spoons.

When they finished their drinks they would fill their cups with beef stroganoff. After one finished the stroganoff they would again refill their cups with their choice of beverage. It was apparent to everyone that it was easier to reuse the same cup as many times as possible to cut down on the need to wash utensils. There wasn't a lot of hot running water for cleaning dishes.

Tom looked around and asked if anyone wanted to play a game of chess. Harry suggested that nobody humor him but Kurt said he would give it try. Juan said he could switch tents with Kurt and moved his sleeping bag over to where Marcy was. Kurt moved his bag to Tom's tent. Tom was heard asking Kurt if he had played before. Kurt indicated he had, but had not played in a long time.

Brad said he had never slept in a sleeping bag before and wondered what he should wear.

Todd said, "Not your boots."

Juan suggested to Brad loud enough for everyone to hear, "You will be warm enough. You can strip down to your underwear or sleep with your pants on. Sleep on your damp socks and they will be dry in the morning. By the end of the trip you will smell so bad you won't have to use insect repellant when we get to the coast."

Marcy moaned, "I need a bath already."

Roy stood at the entrance to his tent. At ten o'clock the sky above was still light but the mountains to the west were dark silhouettes. The glacier was flat grey and to the east glacier blended in with the blue-black horizon. Hushed conversations turned to whispers and the tents grew quiet. Cold air descending the ice-falls and cliffs to the west pressed down the glacier like a silent river current, freezing the water in pots and bottles and bonding them to the surface of the glacier.

The snow that had softened and melted in the sun during the day turned to crystals. Each night the crystals from the previous night grew larger and smoothed over by the melt of the day. The water melting on the cliffs during the day and flowing under the glacier to lubricate their slow movement to the ocean froze. The glacier paused in th stillness.

CHAPTER 3
DAY 2

Roy awoke to the early rays striking the summits of the peaks, dressed and went over to Marcy's tent. Juan heard Roy's boots crunching the frozen snow and crawled out of the tent. "She snores!"

Juan and Roy were the first ones up. They refilled the gas stoves, pumped up the pressure and lit them, then adjusted the flame to a loud purring sound with an intense blue color. They deliberately banged the pans on the stoves and talked louder as they scrambled eggs, fried bacon, made pancakes and boiled water for coffee and tea. The others slowly emerged from their sleeping bags and tents with assorted grunts and groans. One by one they held their plates out for the morning offering. Raymond, Ralph, Michael and Ian ate sitting down while the others stood.

Ralph finished and put his plate on the snow outside his tent. Roy called the plate to everyone's attention. He stressed the need for keeping everything as neat and organized as possible. Living conditions were cramped. Items left lying around could get blown away in the wind or stepped on, get lost in the snow or slide down the slightest icy slope. A pair of gloves set down carelessly might slide away or get blown away putting a person at risk of frostbite.

Grant interjected, "Just like the office, everything has its place." Nobody felt energetic enough to respond.

Breakfast was finished. Everyone finished tea or coffee and wiped their cups clean. They put them into nylon stuff sacks and on top of their sleeping bags in their tents.

Roy held up his crampons and called everybody to get their crampons and gather round. "These things clip onto your boots almost like ski boots onto ski bindings. Put your boot toe into the front bar, put the heel latch on top of the heel and push the latch lever forward. The camming action locks the boot into the crampon so that the boot now has ten one-and-half-inch spikes sticking down from the sole and two spikes sticking out from the toe.

"Walk around for a few minutes like a duck with your legs spread apart a little. I don't want you to step on your own toes or hook your pant legs with one of the points. You are going to have to pay attention when you are standing next to someone not to stab them. DO NOT step on a rope with your crampons. You can cut the rope. You should be able to list a bunch of other don'ts."

Todd said, "Don't step on a sleeping bag." James, "Water bottle."

Michael, "My budget."

Harry responded, "What difference would it make, your estimates are always so full of holes, a couple more wouldn't make a difference."

"Okay Mike and Harry, you are making my job a little easier." Roy said. One of the first things we have to do is divide up into teams of three. Mike and Harry you are together. Marcy you are with them."

"Why?" Marcy asked, "They want to do each other in, why should they take me with them?"

"This climbing thing is sort of crazy," Roy suggested. "It is kind of hard to take out the other guy on the rope without doing yourself in. Self-preservation should keep everyone working together. Michael and Harry will not do anything stupid. If they do they get latrine duty. So here is the lineup: Team 1 is Michael, Harry and Marcy. Team 2 is Raymond, Ralph and Ian, Team 3 is James, Tom and Brad. Team 4 is Eugene, Todd and Grant."

Roy circulated among the three-person groups, asking them to put on their harnesses and to connect them to the climbing rope A loop was tied into the ends of the ropes and in the middle. The loops were connected to the harness with a locking carabineer; an oval chain-link-shaped device with one side that was hinged to open enough that a rope loop could be connected. A nut screwed over the hinge would lock the hinge closed.

Kurt shouted loudly enough for everybody to hear, "When we travel on a glacier we keep the rope as taut as possible but not so much so that you pull the others off balance. With no slack in the rope if one person drops into a crevasse they cannot fall in very far.

"Okay lets start walking toward that hill over there. Be careful to not step on the rope."

For the first half-hour the scene was that of four tug-of-war contests moving up the glacier. One person or another was complaining about a team member walking too fast or too slowly. Over a period of fifteen to twenty minutes the members of each team found a pace that allowed them to coordinate their movements.

Roy moved from team to team and indicated that they were at an altitude of four thousand feet. The air was a little thinner and some might get tired faster than they expected because of the reduced oxygen. He indicated there was trick that mountain climbers used called the "rest step" and gave each team a demonstration.

"When you are walking uphill, put all your weight on the downhill foot. Lock your knee back under the hip. That will take the pressure off your muscles. Also, let the uphill leg go limp and relax it. To take a step, take a breath. As you are sucking in air, shift your hips forward over the uphill foot tighten the muscles of the uphill leg and lift up with your more powerful thigh muscle. As you are lifting your body up, shove the hip of the downhill leg forward and stomp that foot into the snow. That leg now becomes the uphill leg. Rock back on the downhill leg and lock your knee. Relax the uphill leg. Breathe again.

"The stomping of the foot into the snow will form a little platform and your foot is less likely to slip. It also seems to stir up the blood a little and keeps your foot warm. You should be able to travel uphill for several hours at a time without stopping. It will take a few hours to make this a natural process so don't worry if you don't get the hang of it right way."

"Breath, forward, relax. Breath, forward relax," Roy chanted. "I want you all to say it while you are moving up the hill."

Juan remarked to Roy as Roy passed by, "I always like this part. It sounds like a Hindu Mantra. Breathe, forward, relax. You need to throw in 'Oh-o-o-mm.'"

Roy shook his head and muttered, "Irreverent staff I have 'Oh-o-o-mm.'"

The pace slowed down while everyone worked on the breathing and moving sequence. After a while they moved smoothly without chanting. A comfortable forty minutes passed before Roy stopped them.

"Good work gang. You are starting to look like real pros. Let's take a break. Drink some water, snack a little and look at your maps. Get oriented. Use your compass but don't rest them on your ice axe. The magnet in the compass will point to the metal head of the ice axes and you will follow yourself in big circles. Right-handed people will go counter clockwise and left-handed people will go clockwise!"

"Are we supposed to believe that?" Marcy asked.

"Think about it," Roy answered. "Okay, we've been going for about two hours and we are only a little ways up this hill. Everything out here is in such scale and there are no trees or other reference points for size or distance. That rock over there looked about the size of a basketball from camp. From here it looks more like

a railroad boxcar. That icefall over there", he continued pointing toward a low spot, "is between two peaks
where a glacier moved over a cliff and tumbled to the
valley below and then reformed as a continuous flow
of ice. It is ten to eleven miles away."

Tom Gilmore quipped, "That is nonsense. It
can't be more than two miles. It's like looking at a
boat on the horizon."

"James," Roy asked, "do you know how to read a
map?"

"Sure, we all do. That is one of the things we do.
Teach computers how to read and display maps."

"Okay then, from your topography map, if we
are here," Roy pointed to a spot on James's map,
"how far is it to here?"

"You're right," James said, "that is over ten miles
away."

"And that icefall is over five thousand feet high,"
Ian said while he showed Raymond and Ralph the
altitude lines on the map."

"Okay, Juan and Kurt, let's round up these dog-
gies and head them toward that corral over there."
Roy pointed to the slope and ice face that he and
Kurt had explored the night before.

Juan took the other three teams to the sloped
area. Juan would show them the techniques of self-
arrest, sitting hip belay, and boot and axe belay.

Kurt and Roy took James, Tom, and Brad to the
top of the ramp with the vertical drop. Two bollards,

small columns of ice, were cut from the glacial surface and anchor ropes tied to them. James, Tom and Brad were shown how to belay. Sit in the snow, stomp places in the snow to brace their feet about three feet apart to form a tripod. Pass the climbing rope around their waist so that the rope going over the cliff passed within the triangle of their feet and hips, and then around their hips. The belayer on top could control the movement of the rope and, in effect, become an anchor by wrapping the rope around their body.

The further around the belayer's body the rope passed, the more friction was generated. One wrap around the body, especially with a wet rope, was sufficient to hold one or even two people.

Roy said, "Okay, Brad, Tom is going to lower you over the cliff and down thirty feet. I'm going to rappel down and meet you. There I will show you how to climb up the rope by yourself; we will find out how to get help from someone else."

Brad's response was not unexpected, "Why me? Why don't you throw Tom off first, or even James?" He looked at James, "Nothing personal, mind you, but why should I go first?"

Kurt said, "You are on the end of the rope and closest to the edge. We all have to go sooner or later. You might as well go now."

Roy checked the knots on Brad's harness as well as the carabineer lock. Roy also placed an ice axe on the edge of the cliff so Brad's rope would slid on the axe handle and not cut into the edge of the snow cliff and become jammed. He secured the axe with a line to one of the bollards.

"Okay, Brad, lie down here and slide off." Roy led Brad to edge and helped him kneel, then put his feet over the edge. Tom let a little rope slide through his gloves and Brad started to slip over the edge.

"Wait," Brad screamed, "don't drop me. Tom don't let the rope slide! No!" Tom let out some more rope. Brad's waist slipped over the edge and Brad clawed at the edge of the slope with his fingers. "Mother of God," he whimpered, and grabbed the rope in front of him as his body slipped off the edge. "Mother of God, don't let this happen!" he shouted. The people in the other teams looked up and saw Brad hanging from the rope over the edge of the cliff. They looked shocked. Then they heard Brad scream, "Tom, you son of a bitch, don't let me fall, you son of bitch!" They saw him descending slowly from the top.

There was a sudden change in Brad's voice. "Hey, Tom, let it go faster, this is great."

Brad looked to his left and saw Roy hanging from a line, like a spider, next to him. Roy asked him, "How are you doing?" Then he yelled up to the team above, "Kurt, that is far enough." Brad's descent stopped. He looked down.

"Oh, shit. We're not all the way down yet."

"That is true," Roy said casually, and the trick now is to get back to the top."

"Wait a minute." Brad closed his eyes. "I don't believe this. Don't tell anyone. I think I wet my pants."

Roy started to laugh. "No you didn't. You got snow inside your parka when you went over the edge and its starting to melt. You did fine. Besides, the shouting was a good breathing exercise."

"Now let your belayer, Tom, know that you are getting ready to climb up the rope."

Brad looked up. He saw only the white snow in front of him and blue sky above. He said hesitantly, "Tom, I'm coming up the rope."

"Brad," Roy tapped him on the shoulder, "this isn't a board meeting. You are in charge down here and you have to let the guy on top know, in no uncertain terms, what you are going to do. Shout! Suck in some air and really tell him."

Brad looked up again. He shouted as loud as he could. "Tom, I'm coming up the rope." He coughed twice and whispered to Roy, "I've never shouted that hard before. It hurts."

"Altitude is drying out your throat. You'll be okay." Roy reached down and removed the ascender from his harness. "You have one of these on your harness. Get it and place it on the rope above you, as far as you can reach. Like this." Roy attached his ascender to the rope. Brad mimicked his action.

"The ascender will slide up the rope but will not slide down. It is like a portable ladder. Now, slip the loop at the end of the small line attached to the ascender inside the rope around your waist then under your right foot. Like this." Roy raised his knee to his chest and placed a loop around his foot. "Be careful, don't stick your hand with a crampon spike. Then stand up on the loop."

"This is tiring." Brad missed his foot with the loop twice before securing it. "Now what?"

"Clip that diamond-shaped device on your harness onto the rope and sit down. It works like the ascender in that it will slide up the rope but not down. When you sit on it you can push the ascender up the rope. First, you will have to stop standing. Then you can raise it." Roy demonstrated. He sat on the harness, raised the ascender, stood up while moving the harness up the rope, and sat down. In one effortless motion he was two feet higher up the rope. "Try it."

Brad raised his ascender and sat down. He started to gasp for breath. He started to raise the ascender a second time. It didn't move. "It's stuck. It won't go up." His voice cracked with anxiety. He pushed at the ascender.

"Whoa. Stop pushing." Brad continued to struggle, deaf to Roy's voice in his own concentration on the ascender. Roy grabbed Brad's arm and shook him. "Listen to me, Brad!" Roy shouted at him. Brad relaxed. "Brad, you are still trying to stand on the loop. Pull your foot up before you raise the ascender."

"Oh!" Brad raised his foot and the ascender moved up with little effort. Brad repeated the process a few more times while Roy instructed him and then moved up the rope on his own.

"Now what do I do?" Brad had reached the point where the rope went over the edge and he couldn't raise the ascender.

"A number of people have died trying to get out of a crevasse. This is where they have their problem. You have to remove the ascender from the rope and put it back on the rope on the other side of the edge. There are a couple of ways to do it but for this exercise let's call in the troops."

Roy called up to Kurt, "We need a bulgari loop."

The end of a climbing rope with a loop tied in it dropped from over the top of the ice cliff. It knocked a pile of snow onto Brad's head.

"Better snow than a rock," Roy said as he reached the loop, tucked it in inside Brad's harness and placed it around Brad's left foot.

"Okay, James, secure the line," Roy instructed. "Tom, you are doing a great job. You guys make a good team. Hang on for another minute or two." Roy looked at Brad. "You realize, don't you, that Tom has been holding the line to keep you from falling all the time we have been down here?"

"I really hadn't thought about it. What do I do now?" Brad looked at Roy, then at the loop on his left foot.

Roy spoke in a firm monotone. "You will stand up on your left foot. On the line they just dropped. Then you can raise you right foot to take the pressure off the ascender. Then you will disconnect the ascender and place it on the rope on the other side of the edge.

Okay, do it now. Stand on your left foot."

Brad stood up and his head popped up above the edge of the cliff. He saw Tom sitting in the snow holding the rope that he had been hanging from for the past twenty minutes.

Next to Tom was James. He was sitting in the snow in the belay position holding the rope that Brad was standing on. Brad smiled.

"Now, push on the ascender and raise your right foot and stand on the loop." Roy waited. When he saw Brad standing in the right loop he yelled, "Brad, raise your left foot. James, pull in the slack." He could hear Kurt explain to James how to pull in the slack rope and then secure it by wrapping the rope around his waist. "Now Brad, stand on your left foot and raise your right foot."

Brad raised his right foot and pushed on the ascender. When he stood on his right foot he was high enough on the rope to flop his stomach onto the flat surface of the top. He lay there for a few seconds with his head resting on the snow and said, "Piece of cake. I owe you guys my life. Thanks." He lay there for a few more seconds.

Tom sat watching Brad. "You okay? Can I take you off belay?"

Roy worked his way over the edge and said, "Brad, you have to tell them you are secure by saying, 'belay off.'"

Brad looked up. "I'm beat. Belay off." He crawled to his knees and stood up and went to Tom and James and shook their hands. "Thanks again." He looked at Kurt and shook his hands and thanked him. Turning to Roy he said, "I've never done anything so hard in my life."

Roy said "Why don't you guys take a fifteen minute break, snack or take a nap, or do push-ups. I'm going down to see how the others are doing. When I come back, Tom you will go over and then James."

Roy hiked down to where Juan had the other three teams practicing belaying and self- arrests. He remembered his first climbing trip. It was up Mt. Olympus in the Olympic range in Washington State. He was descending the snow dome on the Blue Glacier. From the top he could not see the bottom. The smooth snow slope just got steeper and steeper. He sat on his parka to do a sitting glissade, which seemed a fancy term for sliding down on the seat of your pants. Within seconds he was going faster than he wanted and stabbed at the snow with his ice axe. The ice axe stuck in the snow and jerked loose from his grasp. He slid to the bottom. There were no cliffs or rocks in his path so nothing bad had happened. He had to climb up two hundred feet to retrieve the ice axe. Later in the summer he met someone who showed him how to use the ice axe properly to stop falling.

He watched someone sliding rapidly down the steep slope. It looked like Marcy. She was on her back going down headfirst. She was sliding fast enough that snow flew into the air from her heels as they pressed into the slope. She held her ice axe across her chest. The head of the axe was in her right hand near her shoulder, point up. Her left hand held the bottom of the shaft near he left hip.

In one smooth motion she leaned forward slightly, stabbed the point of the axe head into the snow near her right hip, and swung her feet to the left. She was pulled onto her stomach as the point of the axe grabbed at the snow like an anchor and the momentum of her body carried her down. Her feet swung under her. She was now on her stomach going down the slope feet first. She spread her feet and arched her back forcing her toes into the snow. Her body weight pushed the pick of the ice axe into the slope. She stopped.

"How is everybody doing?" Roy approached Juan. Raymond, Ian and Grant were lined up at the top of the slope, crouching with their backs to the dropoff. Roy could hear Todd yelling, "Get ready, get set..." He was holding his hat in the air.

"They are doing great. Acting like a bunch of kids. Watch this." Juan pointed to the three. "They are having competitions now to see who can get down to those packs first then stop in the shortest distance. They learn fast and seem to be having fun. So far Marcy has beat out all the guys. I think her parka is smoother or something."

"Good. When the team above finishes we should head back to the tents. Tomorrow we should be able to run these teams through the crevasse rescue drill. Also, pick one of these teams to train Tom, Brad and James in the self-arrest."

The summer sun warmed rocks held in place by ice. Periodically there would be a loud thump, crash and clatter as an avalanche occurred somewhere in the valley surrounding them. The first few times they would all stop whatever they were doing and look around. Sometimes they could locate the cascade of ice and rock. From time to time someone would be looking up at one of the icefalls when an avalanche started and would call out, "There goes a big one." Five to ten seconds later the roar of the avalanche would arrive. The distances involved slowly became apparent. As the afternoon passed the sound of avalanches became part of the scenery and didn't draw their attention.

A cold evening breeze was drifting down from the giant cliff to the south as they marched into camp. It was already 9:30 and the sun was still shining on the summits but the valleys were in shadows.

"Ian," Juan said, "tonight you get the honors of being chef. Marcy and Raymond, can you help him with the stoves and water for coffee?"

Grant and Harry offered to help and filled the larger pots with snow. The area south of the cooking was set off for gathering snow.

The latrine area was west about thirty feetof the tents. There was a large crevasse that opened up another thirty feet to the west of the latrine and expanded the length of it in a southerly direction. Where it first opened up, to the right it was only a few inches across. It expanded in a narrow "V" pattern and was three to four feet wide, twenty feet to the left. It eventually opened to a width of twelve feet and appeared to be over a hundred feet deep.

Roy or Kurt would throw the garbage bags into the void of the crevasse. Everyone was warned to stay away from the edge unless they were roped up. As a precaution Roy stretched a rope across the path that would lead to the crevasse and propped it up with ski poles. Juan placed a sign on the rope that read "No Sleep Walkers."

With few exceptions those who were not cooking dinner had crawled into their tents to lie down and rest. Their legs and boots stuck out the tent opening to avoid tracking snow onto their sleeping bags. Muffled conversations grew silent.

Ian placed the contents of the freeze-dried dinners into the boiling water of two large pots and stirred. Two more stoves were used to boil water for drinks and eventually dish washing. Marcy peeled cucumbers and Raymond shredded lettuce and sliced tomatoes.

There were fresh vegetables for the first three days. The prepared vegetables were placed in a clean garbage bag and shaken. Roy indicated he first used the garbage bag salad technique to keep the sand out out of the salad while camping in sand dunes. He indicated he even used the technique at home if he had to toss salad for more than five or six people.

"Dinner's ready!" Ian yelled. Juan, Kurt, Roy and Marcy walked over to the serving area with their plates. "Where is everyone?" Ian asked.

Marcy said, "They are all asleep. I'll get them." She went from tent to tent and kicked the boots of the sleepers. "Dinner," she said each time she kicked a boot. "I am going to use this technique when we get back to the office. When you guys don't get the time sheets and budget authorizations in on time I'll give you a good swift kick. I might have to aim a little higher though."

"Just what we need. A FAWA," Ian said. "What's that?" Juan asked.

"A Female Accountant With Attitude," jibbed Ian.

Her technique worked. Everyone got out of their tents with their plates, spoons and cups.

Roy made a general announcement. "You should all put some water in your water bottles and take them to bed with you. You have worked hard all day and we are at a higher altitude than you are used to and probably a little dehydrated. If you get a headache, drink some water. Other than that there are no other events for the evening. See you in the morning."

Roy, sipping a cup of coffee said, "Juan, Kurt, lets get together in a few minutes up there," pointing to a small knoll a short distance from camp, "and review the how the day went." When he finished his coffee he put the cup in his tent and walked over the slope to where Kurt was sitting. Juan arrived from the area of the outhouse and sat down. The edge of the knoll blocked the view of camp.

Roy looked at Kurt, "What do you think? Any weak links?"

"We are not doing the Eiger or anything like that so extreme strength and technical skill is not required." Kurt glanced at Roy then continued to scan the horizon and the twinkle of stars emerging from the still-lighted evening sky. The reflection off a satellite was a little brighter than the brightest star. "James Wallace is a little weaker than the others.

His older brother, Raymond, is in good shape. Todd Malcolm is a little softer than most. Harry Kuznets is weak. Grant Barnsworth is weak. Tom Gilmore is weak. They all seem to try hard."

"Juan, what are you observations?" Roy asked.

"I agree. James, Todd, Harry and Grant are the weakest but shouldn't have too many problems. I did not see enough of the others to have a feeling about their condition. The thing I notice is that the Wallace brothers do not seem to like each other that much. That Marcy is tough. I bet if Kurt snores she will throw him out of the tent." He looked at Kurt with a smile.

Kurt looked back with a blank stare. "Something else I can't tell about. There is something going on between Tom and Ralph and Grant and Ian. Weird vibrations."

"From what I saw at their office," Roy interjected, "they are in traditional mortal professional combat. One of the things that the old man wants is for these guys to do something together that doesn't involve office turf. If they do, maybe the element of coop-eration will carry over into the office. Nice thought."

"What if they do go after each other?" Kurt asked.

"Separate them by one-hundred and fifty feet of rope. I doubt one would jump into a crevasse just to drag the other guy in. This is our turf, not theirs. With a little luck we can keep them too tired to do anything foolish. But keep your eyes open."

"How about Michael?" Roy asked.

"In the middle physically," Kurt answered.

"He seems isolated from the others," Juan added.

"I think the weather is going to get bad tomorrow." Juan was looking at the sky. "Why?" Kurt asked.

"Those high cirrus clouds coming from the south. Usually at this time of year they mean a front is coming in. That mountain is blocking the view to the south so it is hard to tell." Juan looked at his feet and added, "And my bunions hurt."

"Ah yes, truth," Roy laughed and rose to head back to camp. "Shall we go?"

CHAPTER 4
DAY 3

Marcy heard the wind ripple across the outside of the tent. The sky was already light but the sun was not above the horizon of the ridge to the east. Propping herself on her elbows she looked over at Kurt's sleeping bag. It was a mummy bag and it was pulled over his head. His back was toward her and she could not tell if he was awake or asleep. Had he whispered to her during night or did she dream it. If hc had she could not remember what he said. She also thought it strange that her bag was unzipped. Maybe she had been thirsty and had gotten up to have a drink of water.

The wind rustled the tent again. Marcy crawled out of her sleeping bag and opened the tent zipper. The sky had turned to a grey flat ceiling that covered the tops of the surrounding peaks. The sound of metal hitting metal startled her. Peering around the corner of the tent she saw Roy was stirring a cup of coffee. She pulled on her wool pants and her boots, grabbed her parka, slipped out of the tent and closed the zipper.

"Good morning, I think," she said quietly putting on her parka as she approached Roy.

"Good morning. What do you mean, you think? A grey sky doesn't bother you, does it? Where's your cup? She pulled it from her parka pocket. He poured powdered coffee into the cup and added hot water while they stood.

"Is it going to rain?" she asked as she sipped from the cup and noticed that four stoves were all on and pancakes were cooking in two of them.

"Not until later this afternoon." He added, "We have time for a full day. Your team will have a chance to climb the rope. Let's wake up the rest of the gang and get started. Bang on a pot and rattle their cages."

Roy watched the camp awaken like butterflies emerging from a cocoon. A tent flap would open and one foot would emerge. An arm connected to an unseen person would put a boot on the foot and lace up and tie the boot. The second foot would emerge and the boot would be placed, laced and tied. The feet would turn over, toes down, and the body would back out, stand up and stretch.

Ian was the first out. He already had an aluminum plate in his left hand. For his first few steps he was slightly bent over from stiffness. He walked up to Roy and grunted, "Good morning. Man, I'm stiff."

Roy smiled and answered, "Good morning to you. Hold out your plate. Do you want two or three pancakes?"

"Two."

"Here. There are scrambled eggs on the last stove." Roy dropped two pancakes on his plate and pointed with the spatula to the large pot on third stove to his right. "Butter, syrup, salt and pepper are on the ledge on the other side of the water pot."

"Watch," Roy said, "as everyone comes out of the tent they greet the new day ass first."

Ian walked over to the egg pot and put eggs between his pancakes, buttered the pancakes and squeezed syrup from the plastic container. He set his plate on the snow and took his cup from his parka pocket. He spooned powdered coffee into his cup. As he started pouring hot water into his cup Grant walked by and kicked snow onto Ian's pancakes.

"Hey, retread, watch were you are walking," Ian said.

"Oh! I am sorry. I didn't mean to do that. If you would put things in their proper place accidents like this wouldn't happen." Grant looked at Ian and smiled.

"Accident my ass, you did that on purpose."

Roy asked in a quiet voice looking at Grant, "Two or three pancakes?"

Juan looked over to Roy, "Hey Boss, what was that about? What did he mean retread?"

"Not sure, but I hope their friendliness isn't contagious."

Juan watched as two more people emerged from their tents and walked over. "Let me help you get more pancakes going."

After breakfast the teams reformed and hiked out to the practice site of the previous day. The three people on each rope team moved together. When the first person got to the top of a steep slope he did not start walking faster but kept the same pace until the last person on the rope reached the top. On the previous day the first person up would start to walk faster on the flatter surface and pull the second person off balance. Sometimes the second person would fall over pulling the first person back toward the steep section. This morning they worked as a team.

Apart from a few comments about stiff muscles there were no complaints. The climbing up the rope, belaying and self-arrest exercises proceeded at a methodical pace. By two- o'clock the grey ceiling had lowered to a point where it was not possible to see the cliff guarding the southern end of their valley. The air was crisp. There were no sounds except the occasional clatter of rocks and ice falling somewhere. With no direct sunlight the glaciers in the distance took on a grey-brown tint.

At three o'clock a few drops of rain fell, then increased in intensity, and then mixed with snow. The teams headed for camp. By the time they reached the tents the rain had turned to all-snow. Every one scrambbled to put the rain cover over their tents. Roy had Tom move his sleeping bag into the tent with Kurt and Marcy. Juan moved into Roy's tent.

The vacated tent became the cooking tent.

The intensity of the storm increased. Every half-hour or so somebody had to get out and push the snow away from their tent. The buffeting of the wind made it impossible to hear conversations in other tents. While Roy was out clearing snow from his tent he could hear snatches of conversations from a couple of tents. Michael Kirby seemed upset with James Wallace's reason for moving so slowly on approving Kirby's request to produce the new virtual display in-house instead of having production done in California.

Roy remembered some conversations he'd had during his visit to Wallace Images. Kirby had threatened to leave Wallace Images if he couldn't produce in-house. His file indicated he had gone to MIT for a summer program on production engineering. He had done so to better understand what would be required in setting up a production room. He said he was tired of seeing the profits from his ideas going to another subsidiary that actually produced products.

The wind shifted and he heard Brad say to Grant, "When I went off that cliff yesterday I thought I had peed in my pants. I had never been so scared in my life." They both laughed hysterically.

Roy cooked dinner and carried the pot of Beef Stroganoff from tent to tent while Juan carried the water for coffee and tea. Each person ladled some of the rehydrated food into a bowl and stared at it. Roy would say, "Enjoy."

During the night two feet of snow fell. Kurt was out of his tent just before the first hint of sunrise turned the black of night into a rose tint. He yelled loud enough to wake everyone. Two tents were completely covered and pushed down onto the sleepers inside. He scraped the snow off one, dug down to the zippered opening and opened the tent. Raymond and Eugene looked at him. Raymond said, "What's wrong?"

Roy got out of his tent as soon as he heard Kurt and still barefooted started to dig out Ian and Ralph's buried tent with his hands. When he got to the zipper and opened it Ian and Ralph looked like they were asleep. He shook both of them at the same time. then opened their sleeping bags. Ian and Ralph coughed and choked at being startled awake from a stupor. Roy yelled out, "Kurt, thanks. A few more minutes and we might have had a problem in here."

Ian complained about a headache. Roy explained that they hadn't kept their tent clear of snow and had nearly suffocated. If Kurt hadn't gotten up to clear his tent and seen them buried they might have died.

All the tents were cleared of snow and everybody went back to sleep.

DAY 4

"This will be a lazy day," Roy said to Juan and Kurt. The three were sitting on backpacks, sipping coffee. It was 6:30 AM and the sun was shining on the new snow on the glacier to the north. The crevasses were filled with blue shadows. "Everybody has worked hard for two days at this altitude and their bodies will need time to adjust. They also lost some sleep last night. Let's let them sleep in."

Kurt added, "Traveling today would be dangerous with the snow covering the crevasses."

"The hot sun will settle the snow by tomorrow. Then we will start moving west." Roy indicated he wanted to go north to the glacier that moved east to west, following it west to the base of LaPerouse. From there they would climb to a saddle between LaPerouse and Mt. Marchainville, then head northwest to the south Lituya glacier.

"It should take us two days to get to the base of LaPerouse. If we find a convenient place to practice ice climbing on the way we will stop for half a day. Otherwise, we will practice when we get there."

Juan pointed up the hill to the east of the tents. "Whose tracks are those?" he asked, looking at the trough in the two feet of snow where someone had walked.

"Mine," said Kurt. "I went up to get some pictures of camp in the snow."

The morning sun warmed the snow higher on the peaks and ridges. The snow grew denser as it warmed and softened. The dark rocks absorbed the solar energy. The snow near the rocks melted. By ten o'clock the clattering of small avalanches started like a time bomb ticking. Marcy and Brad were out of their tent, drinking coffee and scanning the horizon. The others were still in their tents. Michael could be heard telling James why they had needed to build a clean room for crystal assembly. Ian seemed to recover from his headache and was writing in a journal some ideas for integrating production data with a virtual operations simulator. Ralph was talking to Raymond indicating he didn't want to talk about it because too many people could hear.

Tom and Eugene were playing a game of chess on a plastic board with regular chess pieces. Eugene suggested to Tom that he get a small magnetic board. "You wouldn't lose pieces. Playing with a bottle cap for a king is a little gauche."

Roy looked at Juan and said, "The tranquility of this group will be shattered soon by Mother Nature."

Juan looked at him quizzically, "What do you mean?"

Roy smiled and said, "Just wait." and sipped at his coffee.

A few minutes later a dull rumbling sound broke the silence and quickly grew louder. The crushing sound rushed down from the giant cliff to the south and grew in intensity until it was a deafening roar.

The new snow at the top of the two-mile high peak slipped off the warming rocks and fell to the next ledge knocking the night's accumulation of snow into space. In a matter of seconds the small cascades grew to an avalanche that covered the face of the cliff.

Thousands of tons of snow and ice raced to the bottom of the cliff and down into the valley hidden from camp by a shoulder of the ridge above them.

Everyone stumbled out of their tents and looked around as if trying to decide which way to run. They looked at Roy, then in the direction of the sound, then back to Roy.

Raymond yelled at Roy, "For god's sake, man, what do we do?"

Roy said, "Relax." A blast of chilled air swept around the shoulder of the ridge and shook the tents. "It was a big avalanche but not big enough to get down here. All the snow from last night became unstable as the sun warmed it. There will be a few more avalanches but none that big."

"Now that I have your attention;" we are going to relax today. This afternoon I want to pack things and get ready to start hiking early in the morning. We want to travel as far as possible before the surface gets too soft. The sun will melt a lot of snow and consolidate it. Over the next few days the surface will firm up and we will be able to travel further. Since the storm has passed we can abandon the cook shack and Tom and Juan can go back to their old tent combination."

Later in the afternoon Roy indicated to Juan that he wanted to talk. They walked a few hundred feet from camp. "Juan, I'm going to scout the route and try to locate the first cache of supplies that was dropped. There is a radio there that I want to get. I'll be back before it's time for everybody to get up in the morning."

Back in camp Roy told Kurt and the rest of the group that he was going to scout the route for the next day and would be back before they had to leave. It would be easy traveling and there shouldn't be any trouble. Roy indicated that Juan was in charge while he was away.

Roy took his daypack, a rope and his ice axe and started north toward the westerly flowing glacier. He started slowly, letting his body warm up, and eased into a comfortable breathing rhythm. After a few minutes he increased his pace.

The sky stayed bright enough to read a map without a light until 11:30 PM. The surface of the glacier was still easy to see and seemed to glow even after midnight. The moon rose and was bright enough to cast dull grey shadows.

Roy reached the general area of the airdrop shortly after midnight. He pushed a button on his watch and heard a beep. He turned his body to the north and the beeping sound grew louder as he ran north. A signal detector in his watch had homed in on a transmitting beacon in the supply drop. There were three parachutes and six boxes. The parachutes were several hundred yards apart. Roy gathered up the boxes and stacked them in a single pile so they could be seen from a distance.

One of the boxes was marked so that Roy knew it contained a radio the size of a deck of cards. The signals it sent and received were not very strong and were highly directional. It was designed to bounce a signal off one of the synchronous GEOstat satellites stationed over the northern part of hemisphere. He turned on the radio and pointed it to the bright, star-like object to the north. "Trigger to Gabby. Trigger to Gabby. Do you copy?"

He knew that the *listener* would have to reach his contact and it might take ten to twenty minutes. He placed the radio in standby and put it in his pocket. After covering the boxes with a red cloth he started jogging back toward the camp. It had taken him five hours to get to the drop site.

Twenty minutes later a series of chirping sounds came from the radio. He stopped, faced north and pointed the little radio toward the satellite. "Hello, Gabby."

"Hello Trigger. Need some oats?" The speaker at the other end of the transmission asked.

"No, everything seems okay here," Roy answered. "Just testing the system. We start moving in the morning."

"Well, Trigger, there is a rattlesnake in the bushes."

"What do you mean?" Roy asked.

"Since you landed we have picked up radio transmissions from your area each night. Highly selective, narrow band. The signal appears to contain location coordinates, some direction and time data and a bunch of code we haven't deciphered yet. One of our guys says it looks like CAD coordinates, computer chip design, or some type of data stream. Who is transmitting? You were supposed to be quiet."

Roy answered, "I don't know what is going on. I'll be in touch." Roy turned off the radio and secured it in a pocket in the lining of his parka. He trudged toward the camp at an even pace. The surface of the snow was firm and each step emitted a "crunch-squeak" sound that was absorbed into the night air.

It was light but the sun was not yet shining on the upper peaks when he arrived in camp. When he was still a mile from camp he could see the tents. He thought he saw a figure moving a short distance from the tents. When he arrived in camp he looked for tracks but the surface was too frozen to leave marks.

He crawled into his tent. Juan's bag was in there.

"Hi boss," Juan woke up fast. "How did it go?"

"No problems. How did it go with you?" Roy answered as he took off his boots and crawled into his bag.

"They all had a big discussion. It only took a few minutes before they all started blaming each other for different problems. Just like you said. I'll fill you in when you get up." Juan crawled out of the tent.

"Thanks, Juan," Roy said. "Wake me up in an hour."

Marcy crawled into the tent and shook Roy. He groaned and opened one eye and looked at her. She said, "Here is your morning coffee. Juan said you hiked all night and your hour is up."

"Thanks. I checked the route," Roy said, then added, "how are you doing?"

"Fine." She said. "How could a girl complain about being stuck on an island of ice with a hunk for a tent mate?"

"Nothing serious, I hope." Roy feigned serious-ness. "I don't want you wearing out my staff."

"Don't worry, he is nice to talk to. He is one of the few people I've met who seems to understand my interests. He knows how to listen."

"Boss," Juan stuck his head into the tent, "what time do we break camp?"

"Good question, Juan. Let's try to be on the trail by ten o'clock. We can discuss the art of walking while we travel."

Juan's head disappeared. Roy looked at Marcy, "Sorry, I have to stop listening for a while."

DAY 5

The morning air was crisp and the sun on the ridges reflected off ice-crusted snow. The tents had been taken down and rolled into small packages that went into a backpack. The lightweight tent poles folded and fitted nicely into a side pocket of a backpack. The tents and tent poles were divided among the team. Those who didn't have part of a tent put a stove or cooking pot into their packs. Juan gathered up loose items of debris and threw them into the crevasse next to camp.

Each person stepped into the leg loops of a harness and cinched the waist buckle. A locking carabineer was attached to the two loops that pulled the waist loop around the body. Roy indicated who would be on the ropes together and everybody snapped a loop from the rope into their carabineers. A series of groans was heard as packs were lifted. This was the first time on the trip that they carried full packs weighing forty to fifty pounds. The day packs had been twenty pounds.

Roy said loud enough for every one to hear, "We will travel like we have practiced. Keep the rope in front of you free of slack but don't pull on it. I'll start off." Roy started walking and Ralph uncoiled the rope. When the rope tightened Ralph started to walk and Grant waited until the slack in front of him disappeared. The first team was moving.

Juan started the second rope and followed a few steps behind Grant. Eugene and Todd followed on Juan's rope. Mike, Harry and Marcy then James, Brad and Tom followed them. Kurt, heading the last team walked alongside Tom. While the teams slowly departed, Ian, the last person on the last rope, noted in his journal the composition of the rope teams:

Roy, Ralph, Grant Juan, Eugene, Todd Mike, Harry, Marcy James, Brad, Tom Kurt, Raymond, Ian

The five teams, stretched out over a distance of 750 feet, moved single file to the north.

The fresh snow from two nights before had melted during the previous day and frozen during the night. Now that the sun had been out for a few hours the frozen crust was getting softer. When the teams first started, the crust held the weight of the heaviest person. As they walked the frozen crust softened. For half an hour the walking was difficult because the crust would break under the heavier hiker's feet every few steps. They wouldn't know if their footing would collapse and sink in six to eight inches. The heavier people found it easier to follow in the footsteps of the person in front of them.

The snow softened as the sun rose and everyone sank in to the base of the new snow. Everybody followed in the same tracks. The foot-holes filled with blue shadows.

Roy formed a second set of tracks as he stepped to the side and slowed his pace. Juan's team passed and took the lead. Slowly the other teams came up alongside Roy's team and he could spend a few minutes with each person on the different rope teams. He would walk alongside them and check to see how they were doing with the heavier packs.

Several people noted that the walking was becoming monotonous.

"Put your mind in the numb mode and keep putting one foot in front of the other," Roy suggested to each person. "Don't think about how far we are going or how long it will take." He also suggested that they practice deep breathing. "Focus on your breathing for awhile. Feel the air coming in and going out. Imagine the air coming in and energy moving through your body. Imagine becoming part of the snow."

Roy could hear that Tom Gilmore was breathing hard. Tom was the last person on rope headed by James. "I am glad James is in worse shape than I am," Tom said as he slowly came alongside Roy. "If he went any faster, I would fall down."

Roy said, "Juan is up front. He will make sure nobody goes too fast. Here," Roy offered Tom a water bottle, "Have a drink of water."

"These sunglasses make the snow look brown. Looks like sand. I get the feeling we are walking in the desert," Tom said as he took the bottle. He unscrewed the top and drank two large swallows of water. He didn't miss a step as he put the top back on the bottle and handed it to Roy. "It is hot enough and I was thirstier than I thought. Thanks."

"No problem," Roy answered. He kept pace with Tom. They walked for several minutes. The only sound was Tom's heavy breathing and their boots thumping into the snow. Roy broke the silence. "I understand you are the genius behind the company's products."

"I have had a few ideas."

"You are being modest. Raymond says you're the one who got Wallace Images going."

"You're right," Tom said. "So what does Raymond do? Hang me out to dry. Cuts me off and sticks me in another building, then has his sniveling little brother hire my replacement."

"That's pretty heavy. What do you mean?" Roy asks.

"For the first four or five years I thought he was my best friend. We would kick around ideas and have fun figuring out how to make things work. God, there were times that we be at it until two or three in the morning. That was great. Now I am stuck over in the R&D building and he never comes around. The only time we talk about ideas is when there is a review meeting or some other time when he has Kirby pounding on me about making designs more compatible with production or having Dresner explain new research directions. That's my department, not Dr. Flashy's."

"Whoa!" Roy said, "You make me feel like a dentist who just hit a raw nerve!"

"You asked," Tom started to respond to Roy. Kurt's team had slowly been catching up with the rope that Tom was on. Kurt was now only two steps behind Tom.

"Roy," Kurt said, "Raymond was wondering when we are going to take a break."

"We'll talk some more later," Roy said to Tom. Roy slowed down while Tom and Kurt slowly moved passed him and Raymond approached.

Raymond was fifty-five, tall and slender, and in good shape. He loved running and cross- country skiing.

"This is great, I should have had us do this years ago." Raymond sucked in a long breath.

"Kurt said you were asking about taking a break," Roy said.

"Hell, no. I was wondering how long it would be before my little brother collapsed."

"I'll make sure he doesn't. Sorry to ruin your fun." Roy laughed and slowed down until Ian, the last person on Kurt's rope and the last person in the long line of climbers, caught up with him.

Ian commented as he walked up to Roy, "This is different. Back at the office we push hard all day in one and two-hour increments. A meeting here, a meeting there. Push to get a design idea sketched out and transmitted to someone else.

Review a plan and comment and get on to the next task."

Roy commented, "Here," he said, "we put one foot in front of another and breathe to keep the energy flowing. There is no real deadline."

Ian said, "I find it hard to turn my mind off. Keep thinking about the different things."

"When you get tired enough you will. Pretty soon you will feel you are falling asleep walking. You will start counting the insects that have blown in on the wind. You will see differences in the shade of blue of the shadows in the footprints in front of you."

"Maybe so," Ian said. "For the moment it seems that with each step I think, 'Damn Grant.' Left foot goes down - Damn. Right foot goes down -Grant. It helps keep a rhythm."

"So what is the problem?" Roy asked in a casual way as he thought back to Ian's file folder and the pancake incident at breakfast. Ian had been hired four years before. Wallace Images was in the middle of their last large expansion effort. Ian was hired by James to manage internal operations. The original job description included setting up a net-work of desktop computers and providing support to secretaries and anyone else who needed help processing data.

"Last night he calls me a kid with my toys. I'll be thirty next month. The toys are his problem. The toys, the desktop computers, can run circles around his mainframe and he can't stand it. The mainframe has its place in the design aspect of what Wallace

Images does, but it is not being used for internal communications or project control. That is what James hired me to do."

"What was the retread thing this morning?" Roy asked.

"He has really gone freaky the last year about his computer. He sees it like a temple of ordered activity and proper place. He acts like he has gone through some kind of religious conversion, like a Born Again Christian. It's not really religious. He is just obsessive about neatness and his view of the dominant role of the mainframe. Some of us call him retread behind his back. He knows it."

"He even argues against PC's because he thinks that programming PC's is sloppy and unstructured and that PC data is not secure. Every friggin time I put in a request to network PC's, Grant butts in and gets Kuznets or James Wallace to cancel the funding. I could set up an inventory system for production in five or ten minutes with a good database program that would take him two to three weeks to test. He won't even consider automating inventory control. He thinks it can be done by hand. I can't tell if he just doesn't have a clue or is so paranoid about his design security and Wallace Images proprietary data that he can't think straight. He even pulled payroll activity away from some simple PC applications I had set up. Now all the costing and accounting data is managed by an outside firm. Even the time and attendance records are maintained by the company that provides the time clocks."

Roy interrupted, "Ian, I want to hear about how you can help Wallace Images with your PC's, but I have to check out some of the rope teams."

As Roy passed James he noticed that James was gasping. "Having a problem?"

"I don't know what happened. I was doing fine and suddenly my body gave up."

"You lost your concentration on breathing. Exaggerate sucking in air for while. You will feel better. With practice you will learn to breathe deeply without thinking about it."

Roy called to Juan on the first rope, "Juan, slow the pace a little."

A cheer went up from each rope.

The pace slowed a little and the teams traveled for two hours before Roy called for a break. One by one the members of a rope team walked with a deliberately paced step to the group. The person in front pulled in the rope and made a neat coil. When they were done they let their packs fall off their shoulders into the snow. Most stood for few minutes and shrugged their shoulders, working stiffness out of the muscles, and then collapsed on the snow and lay against their packs.

"I hope I don't have to put that thing on again." Marcy moaned.

Harry smiled as if he enjoyed her discomfort. "This is a man's world."

"Don't give me that macho bullshit. I can tell by your gasping face that you are hurting more than I am and are just afraid to admit it. Is that what macho means? Afraid to admit weakness? Afraid to admit you need help?"

When they first stopped, Juan had packed the snow in front of him into a solid surface, placed a stove on it and started to melt snow. Now Juan approached Marcy and Harry with a pot of hot chocolate. "Care for something energizing?"

Marcy took her cup from a pocket of her pack. Juan filled it. She turned her back to Harry to stare back at the tracks they had made that disappeared over the horizon as she sipped the chocolate.

Roy said to the group, "Before we get started put some extra sun cream under you chin, under your ears, in your nostrils and under your nose. When the sun starts reflecting off the snow in front of us it will burn everything from the bottom side."

Harry looked at Marcy, "Will you help me put my pack on?"

"Geeze, Harry. Are you a helpless wimp? Sit on the ground, slide the straps over your shoulders and stand up. Like a man."

"Damned if you do. Damned if you don't," Harry muttered. "Will I ever learn?"

"With enough time," She answered.

The rope in front of Harry straightened out as Michael started hiking. "Time to break up the contest," He said.

The teams traveled for another three hours before stopping. This was the longest stretch of time that every person had been isolated from the others by the length of the rope. As they stopped and discarded their packs they sat down in the snow. They braced their backs against their packs, closed their eyes and tried to go to sleep.

Roy signaled Juan and Kurt to follow him and hiked up a slight incline away from the group. The three sat looking back at the twelve from Wallace Images sprawled on the snow.

"So how do you think they are doing?" Roy asked as a general question. "Juan, you suggested this morning that the group got heated up a little last night. I've picked up a few vibrations today. Kurt, how do you see our group?"

"They are, what is a good term? Volatile. Volatile, I think is a way to describe them. Michael seems to be a lightning rod of sorts. He is in charge of a major project that has had some setbacks. His boss seems to be, on paper, James. Raymond suggests that James screwed up and didn't do a complete enough job on planning the project. Harry says Michael and James bid too low on the contract and Wallace Images is losing money on every product they sell. Even Todd who seems to be the quiet one suggests that Michael doesn't have the program management software to control the contract. Then Harry says Michael is too bull-headed to use it even if it were available."

Juan interjected, "Then Ian jumps in and says James could probably keep track of Michael's costs, inventory needs and quality control problems if he had PC's networked into the different departments that are affected by the contract. Then Kurt and I had to separate Michael from the others. He was ready to take them all on."

"Like I said, volatile." Kurt added.

"Where was Raymond in all this?" Roy asked.

Juan looked at Kurt, then at Roy and said, "Just sitting back smiling."

"Okay. Let's go start dinner," Roy said as he stood and headed back to the group.

CHAPTER 5
RAYMOND

The sky was clear with no threat of rain or snow. Raymond asked Roy if they could sleep outside the tents. He wanted to watch the stars and see the northern lights. Marcy and Michael indicated they, too wanted to sleep under the stars.

"That should be okay. There are no bears wandering around here. Not too many anyway. You might want to put a plastic sheet over your bag to keep the dew off. Also, you might notice in the morning that you will have more condensation on the underside of the plastic than you have dew on the top. Just make sure you keep your head in the open or all of the moisture in your breath will condense on the underside to the cover."

Marcy asked, "What do you mean, bears?"

"There is a blue glacier bear up here, supposedly a cross between a grizzly and a polar bear.

They seem to head for the coast in the spring and cross this way in the fall on their way to hibernate. I've followed their tracks but have never seen one. We had one go through a camp a few years ago between a bunk tent and the food cache. It left prints a foot across and seemed to step over crevasses eight to ten feet across without difficulty. It must have been huge. It wasn't interested in us then and probably wouldn't be interested in us now. Of course, we didn't have women in camp then."

After dinner was finished the exertion of the day's travelling became apparent. Todd grunted, "I'm beat." He crawled into his tent. Marcy put her foam pad on the snow and the sleeping bag on top of it. She put a plastic cover over the sleeping bag and put some snow around the sides and base to keep the wind from blowing the plastic off. Michael tucked his plastic under the foam pad. Raymond secured the plastic sheet with snow as Marcy had.

The rest of the team crawled into their tents. Tom said he was going to Kurt's tent to play chess since Marcy was sleeping outside. In a few minutes the camp was quiet.

The crunch of snow under James's feet woke Marcy. "Who is that? Is it time to get up already?" She asked. The morning sky was already light enough to cast long, blue-grey shadows over the glacier. The top of Mt. Crillon was washed in a red glow from the first rays of sun.

"No," He whispered, "James. I was visiting the facilities. It is only four-thirty. Everybody is still asleep."

An hour later Roy stuck his head out of his tent. He looked at the other five tents and atthe three sleeping bags on the glacier. "Anybody want coffee besides me?"

Michael sat up pulling the plastic off his bag. "Yuck, I'm soaked," he said running his hand over the wet sleeping bag and under the wet plastic sheet. "Why am I wet?"

Marcy suggested, "You covered your head and the moisture from your breath and evaporating snow condensed on the underside of the plastic."

Michael made a snowball and threw it at Raymond's bag a few feet away. The snowball bounced off the plastic covering Raymond. It hit near the knees. He didn't move.

"Come, you corporate ostrich," Marcy jibbed, "pull your head out from under the plastic and say hello to the morning." She struggled as she pulled her pants on while still in the sleeping bag. She crawled out of the bag, slipped on her boots and walked to Raymond. She knelt and as she put her hand on the plastic cover to shake him an alarm went off in the back of her head. Adrenaline jolted her as she sensed that Raymond might not be breathing. She jerked her hand back.

"Roy," she shouted, "Roy, come here. Hurry."

Roy scrambled from his tent. The urgency of her voice pulled the others from their tents.

Roy knelt and shook Raymond gently, then firmly. He started to slip his fingers under the plastic sheet near Raymond's head and noticed the grip of ice along the edge of the plastic. "Oh-oh." He muttered to himself as he pushed his fingers under the rim of ice and ripped the plastic upward. Raymond's face was pale and there was a blue tinge to his lips. Roy pressed a middle and index finger against Raymond's neck checking for a pulse. The skin was cold and stiff.

"He is dead," Roy said, "suffocated."

Marcy stood up and backed away. She grabbed Kurt who had walked up behind her. "How can he be dead?" she asked, looking at Roy, then Kurt.

Kurt answered, "It looks like he covered his head with the plastic. The condensation on the inside froze and sealed the edge of the plastic to the glacier. It cut off the flow of air under the cover. As he slept he used up all the oxygen. It was painless. A terrible accident."

Grant looked over at James and said, "Well, James, your wish has been realized. Your brother is dead and you are in charge."

James glared at him.

"You heartless son of a bitch," Marcy hissed the words at Grant.

Roy opened the bag to check Raymond's body to see if anything else was unusual. "Juan, get his personal things out of his tent. We'll put them in the bag with him."

James asked, "What do we do with Raymond? Can we call this whole thing off and get out of here?"

"There is not much we can do with him other than cover him up and pack him in snow until we can get back here with a chopper. As for what we do, we have to follow our basic plan to get to the coast. Let's break camp and move as soon as possible. I don't think we all want to be wandering around here."

Silence gripped the camp while the tents were taken down and everyone prepared to continue across the glacier. From time to time someone would stop and stare at the mound of snow that Roy and Juan had built over Raymond's body. They had dug a trench in the glacier surface four feet deep and placed the body in it. They covered the body with a pile of snow four feet above the surface of the glacier.

"Why so much snow?" Tom asked.

"It will melt down in ten to twelve days."

The teams roped up. Roy put Grant on the rope with Kurt where Raymond had been. This left Roy and Ian as a two-man team. The teams left the site in an orderly manner. Each person turned to look at the mound as they walked away.

After half and hour of hiking Roy stopped and signaled Juan to keep moving. When Juan, walking at a disciplined methodical pace reached Roy, Roy started to walk. They were over fifty feet ahead of the Eugene and Ian team and could talk without being overheard.

"Juan, we got a big problem," Roy said without looking around or slowing his pace. "Raymond was murdered. It wasn't an accident."

Juan sucked in a big breath and asked, "How do you know?"

"Did you notice that the ice that sealed the plastic sheet was on the outside of the plastic. Ice from frozen condensation would be on the underside of the plastic. Somebody dripped water along the outer edge"

"Who do you think did it? What are the others going to do when they find out someone is a murderer?"

"We cannot afford to tell them yet. Do you hear me? Don't mention it. I don't what anybody to panic. We have to try to figure out who did it."

"Okay, boss. Mum is the word," Juan acknowledged Roy's request.

They hiked for twenty minutes alongside each other. They were starting a westerly crossing of the Brady glacier. It was nearly twenty miles across. Juan asked, "If someone killed Raymond, will they do it to anybody else?"

"I'm not sure," Roy glanced back at the rope teams. "There is another problem. It might be connected to Raymond's death. I contacted the general last night. He indicates that someone has been transmitting data from our camps every night since we got here."

Juan stopped moving. His stop sent a domino effect back to all the other team members. Everybody stopped. "What is going on?" he asked.

Harry yelled, "Juan, can we take a break? We have been going an hour and still haven't had breakfast."

"I don't know, but keep your eyes and ears open," Roy cautioned Juan. "Don't say anything to the others."

Roy motioned for the others to come forward. They would take out the stoves and prepare coffee and some oatmeal and relax for an hour.

As each person arrived they turned and pulled in and coiled the rope leading to the next person on the rope. When all the members of a rope team had arrived the rope was already neatly coiled. There were no problems with anyone tripping over seven hundred and fifty feet of rope scattered about. When the coils were dropped each person unclipped the rope from their harnesses and took off their packs. The air was still cool. Most of the team took their parkas off their packs and put them on.

Juan and Kurt set up four stoves and started them while Brad and Ian packed snow into the large pots. Todd asked where the latrine was located. Roy suggested he go west about fifty feet. There was a slight knoll in the snow and a person standing there would be out of sight.

A few minutes later Todd came back from over the knoll. Roy said, "Damn, the power of suggestion. Now I have to go." He headed up the knoll. Eugene followed.

"Me, too. You don't mind if we pee on the glacier together do you?"

When they were out of sight of the others Eugene asked, "Did Raymond say anything about why I had been hired?"

Roy indicated that Raymond had not said anything specific. He remembered that several others thought that Eugene had been hired to replace Michael Kirby.

Eugene started to explain. "Raymond approached me two years ago and arranged for me to join Wallace Images. My specialty was chip design and chip manufacturing and I had a lot of experience in converting software to circuits. But that wasn't why he hired me."

Kurt and Tom came over the knoll. Eugene stopped talking, finished relieving himself and walked back to camp followed by Roy. The remainder of the group was in a semi- circle around the stoves. Some sat. Todd was standing. He seemed rigid and had a blank stare. He started to shake gently. When his shaking splashed coffee out of his cup Brad noticed him.

"Todd, what is wrong?" Brad asked, standing and moving toward him. Todd's tremors increased and he dropped his cup.

Todd murmured, "I need a drink. I can't stand it. I need a drink."

Ralph said, "Oh great. The alkie is picking a fine time to come apart."

Roy told Juan to get Todd's sleeping bag. He hugged Todd until the shaking stopped and got him to lie down on the sleeping bag. Juan had opened it wide. When Roy got Todd down he folded the top of the bag over him. Todd said in a low, tight-lipped monotone. "I don't want to die." He tried to throw the cover of the sleeping bag off.

Roy asked Marcy to sit with Todd for a few minutes and try to calm him down. Todd fell asleep.

Kurt and Tom placed Tom's chessboard on a pack and continued the game they had started the night before.

An hour later Roy indicated that they should resume travel. Marcy woke Todd and gave him a cup of coffee. When he finished the coffee, Juan helped him roll up the sleeping bag and repacked it.

Roy signaled Juan and Kurt. The three stood and walked away from the others a few feet. Roy said, "Kurt, I want to take Ralph off my rope so I can move from team to team and keep track of how people are doing. Let's put him where Raymond was as second on your rope."

Kurt gestured that it was okay.

"Juan," Roy said pointing west to the left of Mt. LePerouse, "do you see that Nunatak over there? Head for it in as straight a line as possible. If you have to walk around a crevasse I want you to go to where you would have been if you could have jumped it."

"Okay, Boss. What's a Nunatak?" Juan smiled.

"See that pile of rock, looks like a small peak sticking up from the glacier?" Roy pointed again.

"Got it," Juan said.

The rope teams reformed and Roy headed them west. Juan, Eugene and Todd left first. Michael, Harry and Marcy left second. James, leading Brad and Tom, waited a few seconds for Marcy to pass then started hiking. When Todd started hiking, Kurt moved forward and walked along beside him. Ralph let out the fifty feet of rope before he started and Ian waited. Roy walked alongside Ian and Grant followed Roy.

Roy and Grant had tied onto the rope fifty from the ends of the one-hundred-fifty-foot rope and they were fifty feet apart. If Grant fell into a crevasse, Roy had the fifty-foot end of rope to drop down to him for help.

The intense sun was rapidly melting the snow that had fallen two nights before. Small rivulets flowed down the glacier and joined others. In places the teams stepped over small rivers that were forming on the glacier in the afternoon sun. At one point they passed a crevasse into which a river was flowing. Roy indicated to Ian that there were huge sub-glacial rivers that emerged at the glacier's snout.

Roy looked back at Grant and indicated he wanted to move up to the next team. He picked up his pace and caught up with Ralph. "How you doing?" He said when he was alongside.

"I'm doing okay," Ralph said. "Still a little bummed out by what happened to Mr. Wallace and Todd. Walking along in the middle of a rope sure isolates one. I can't remember thinking about so many things that weren't tied to a project in a long time. I've been thinking about a good friend, Frank, who works for XYCore, another company in our line of business. Actually they are a competitor. I don't know why but every time I think of Frank I get the feeling I've seen Kurt before."

"By the way," Ralph added, "thanks for stopping by. It does get lonely in the middle of the rope. Like middle management I guess. I've noticed that Kurt and Tom have struck up a pretty lively conversation."

Roy increased his pace again and passed Kurt and Tom, said hello, and walked ahead to Brad. "How you doing?" he asked Brad.

"Great, considering." Brad seemed stronger and surer of himself than any other time Roy had talked with him. "How is Todd doing?" he asked Roy.

"Why do you ask?"

"Todd seemed to be coming apart back there. He has had a lot bottled up. Sorry about the pun. His alcohol problem has created some problems at work but mostly at home. His wife is unhappy. Todd sometimes asks if I know of anyone who might be fooling around with her. How do you answer a question like that?"

Roy asked, "Is she?"

Brad hiked a few minutes before answering. "A couple of people have suggested that."

Roy interrupted, "You are covering your tail. When you say 'a couple of people,' what people do you mean?"

"Tom has suggested that he got pictures of Ralph and Todd's wife together at a group trip to the Caribbean last fall. If I saw anything that suggested that Ralph was going to make a play for my job then I could squash it." Brad's confidence seemed to ebb. "The way Todd was acting I wonder if he knows. This is such a mess."

Roy moved up to the next team and reached Marcy. She heard him coming and turned her head in his direction. "How far do we go today?" she asked.

"Another two or three miles," he replied. Pointing he added, "Tomorrow we should be near that peak poking up out of the glacier."

He moved forward. "Hi, Harry."

Harry responded with a grunt, "Can we take a break?"

"That's not a bad idea," Roy responded. He noticed that Juan was approaching the beginning of a major crevasse field. For the next two miles they would be encountering crevasses twenty to forty feet across and one hundred to one-hundred-fifty-feet deep.

Depth was hard to judge because many crevasses opened above older crevasses that had not been closed by glacial movement.

Travel in a straight line would not be possible. The distance around a crevasse might be three-quarters of a mile. Snow and ice bridges existed and looked like the threads con- necting the two sides of a cloth that has been ripped. Some of the bridges were a few feet thick and looked as if they would collapse if anyone walked on them. Others were tens of feet thick. Some of the crevasses revealed large tunnels under the surface, running perpendicular to the crevasse.

Roy called to Juan and told him find a good spot to rest. He wanted the team to get together, to take a break, and review what they would be doing for the next few hours and the next day.

"Michael," Roy yelled, "stay in Juan's tracks." Michael caught up to Juan's team as Roy did so.

"This glacier is a mess," Michael exclaimed walking toward the edge of the crevasse to look in.

Roy saw that Michael was walking onto a thin lip of snow that overhung the crevasse. He grabbed the rope that connected Michael and Harry. He hooked it around his ice axe and plugged the axe into the snow up to the head next to his boot and wrapped the rope around his boot is one swift motion.

"Michael, stop. Get back from the edge!" As Roy was yelling at Michael the snow on which Michael had just stepped collapsed. Michael disappeared.

Marcy cried out, "Where did Michael go?"

The rest of the group turned toward the hole in the snow three feet from the edge of the crevasse. Roy shouted, "Everybody stay where you are! Kurt, Juan see how far down Michael is. Harry, sit down and belay Juan. Ralph, belay Kurt."

Kurt and Juan, four feet apart probed with their ice axes as they worked their way toward the spot where Michael had disappeared. Each took a step and thrust the staffs of their ice axes into the snow in front of them. Their axes sank in twelve inches.

They pulled their axes out and took another step. They were trying to determine where the solid part of the glacier ended and the overhanging snow ledge began. Juan, following in Michael's steps, pushed his ice axe down the full length of the shaft two feet from the edge of the hole.

The lip overhung the crevasse by nearly five feet. He backed up and shouted back to Harry to tighten up on the belay. He lay down on his stomach and inched forward until he reached a point where he again could push his ice axe through the lip. He rotated the staff slowly, carved a hole and peered down. He saw Michael looking back at him. Juan asked, "You hurt?"

"No, but get me out of here." Michael's voice was strained.

"Cover your head while I make this hole a little bigger," Juan said as he cut away the snow that separated his probe hole from the one that Michael had fallen through.

James brought Juan the end of a rope that Brad was belaying. Juan placed his ice axe across the lip of the hole. He tied a loop at the end of the rope with a boland knot and dropped the rope down to Michael. He had to swing it back and forth a few times before Michael could grasp it. To keep the rope from cutting into the edge of the crevasse Juan ran it over the ice axe.

Michael snapped the rope into the carabineer on his chest harness and then stood in the loop that Juan had tied. Standing in the loop took the pressure off the rope that Roy had anchored so that it could be moved and an ice axe placed under it. Kurt lowered another rope with a loop in the end and told Michael to tie his pack to it, then take the pack off. Kurt pulled the pack up and threw it back, away from the hole. Kurt then pulled up on each rope going to Michael as Michael transferred his weight from one rope to the other. In three minutes his head appeared above the hole and he climbed back to the surface.

Juan said, "Piece of cake. Just like we practiced. You did good." He patted Michael on the back as Michael sprawled forward on his stomach on solid snow. Michael looked pleased with his skill in getting out of the crevasse and at the same time foolish for having fallen in.

He asked, "How come I didn't fall in all the way?"

Harry said, "Roy grabbed the rope and put you on belay just as you fell."

Michael shook Roy's hand and said, "You saved my life. Thanks."

Roy suggested that he was just doing what everybody would be doing once they knew how to read the glacier.

"Let's move over there and set up camp, have dinner and discuss glaciers." The group slowly stretched out the ropes and traveled half a mile further across the glacier before stopping and setting up camp. The stoves were turned on and water boiled and meals prepared.

While they ate Roy explained that the glacier was like a like a frozen pizza placed on the kitchen table. "If you put the pizza over a bowl the edges will droop when the pizza thaws, and the center will be higher than the edges.

When the glacier flows over a mountain ridge the center is pushed up and cracks that form are "V"- shaped.

"The top of the crevasse is wider than the bottom. If you place the pizza edges on two bowls with nothing under the middle, the center will droop. When a glacier flows over a valley or large depression the crack is wider at the bottom than at the top. In fact, the crevasse might not even be open at the top. Hidden crevasses are that type. You might not see the crevasse until you fall in. Michael fell into one where the top was already open but it got wider the deeper it went. These often have the appearance of a thin snow bridge."

Roy drank some coffee. "Look at the other side of the crevasse. You can see where there is still part of the bridge that connected to this side."

"From now on don't walk toward the lip of a crevasse unless you are belayed."

"Michael walks around here like he does in the office," Grant said. "Thinks he is in charge and won't listen to anyone. Here he will get killed. There he is killing us all."

Michael glared at him and retorted, "What does that mean?"

"You know that your decision to buy green crystals to speed up the delivery of the Virtual Display Communicator and your not telling anyone about it what is bankrupting the company."

James stared at Grant, then Michael. "Grant, what are you saying?"

"Two years ago when all the Communicators we had shipped came back because of failures in the frequency crystals, Kirby here said we needed a clean room to avoid contamination of crystals during crystal assembly."

Juan asked, "What is a clean room?"

"That has set us back two million dollars," Harry interjected.

Grant added, "The problem was you thought you could knock three months off the time to make the first communicator by buying the crystals from the vendor before their electrical properties had aged and were certified. You got them sooner and cheaper. Made you look good. You didn't tell anyone.

"After the Communicators were built and shipped, the electrical properties of the crystals changed and the Communicators failed. Ian found out when he first got here. He was reviewing the original production plan and comparing it to what actually happened using what he called 'The Critical Path Method' he noticed a three-month difference in the time to get crystals. He asked me why?"

"As I remember, you told me to take a flying.. whatever.. when I asked you. I brought it up with Mr. Wallace. You convinced him that our data was the problem. Out of spite or because you were paranoid you had him pull my organization apart and sent all accounting functions outside. You were trying to cover your tail and ripped apart our ability to get control over our problems."

Michael walked to Grant and put the point of his ice axe up to Grant's throat. "I don't have to take this crap from you now. I didn't take it from you last year and I am not going to let you bad-mouth me now."

Kurt brushed the axe away and stepped between the two. He faced Michael and got him to back away from Grant.

"Ian, Eugene and Ralph have reviewed the project and agree with me," Grant said. He was pale and shaking from the physical confrontation. The adrenalin rush he experienced when Michael put the ice axe to his throat wore off and his knees weakened. He sat down on the snow. "You had Mr. Wallace, kiss-ass Harry and Tom so brainwashed we had to hire Marcy, Eugene and Ian had to try to rebuild internal controls. All this because you couldn't share a decision you made that would affect everyone."

Roy sat quietly during the eruption, sippng his coffee, watching the two square off and the reactions of the others. "Michael... Grant," he said stretching and standing, "let us cool off a little. One of the reasons we are out here is that Mr. Wallace was concerned about internal communications and he hoped some new forms of dialogue might emerge. This is new from what I understand. Whether it is the type of interaction he wanted we will never know."

"While we are at it, does anyone else want to add anything? James? Tom? Brad?" Roy looked at each person as he called their name and waited until they looked back. Each person shook his head.

Michael was glaring at Tom, "You set me up didn't you? You suggested that I could speed up the delivery of crystals. You R&D guys wanted to sabotage engineering. You thought production would reduce the glory of research and development."

Tom, sitting on his pack, looked back and smirked. "You were an idiot then and still are. Wallace Images has been a force because of its research ideas. Other people do a better job of production. You screw up and blame the marketing department for the lack of sales."

Michael started to lunge at Tom but Kurt held him back. "Mr. Wallace knew you were washed up in the idea department and we needed a new business direction. Why do you think Ralph was hired? He knows where R&D fits into the company picture."

Tom looked at Michael, then slowly at Ralph, then back at Michael. "Ralph," he said in a monotone, "knows where he stands in this organization. He gets the picture."

"Don't be so sure," Michael yelled angrily in Tom's direction. "He'll screw you like he did Todd's wife and that teenager in Colorado last year."

The mention of Todd's wife stunned Brad. Brad looked toward Roy. Everybody looked at Ralph, then Todd.

Todd's eyes focused on Ralph for a few seconds. "You," he said, then dropped his head to his chest and started to sob, "I knew it, there was someone. I've been such a failure to her. I didn't want to believe it."

"You!" Marcy said in a whisper. She backed away from the circle and stared across the crevasse-scarred glacier to the west. "You!"

Michael seemed to run out of energy and sat down. Kurt walked away from him and approached Roy. "Keep your eye on Marcy," he said quietly. I'll explain later."

Two hundred feet away there was a loud thumping sound followed by the whoosh of air escaping as ice fragments flew thirty feet into the air. A large snow bridge collapsed and fell into the crevasse below it. The mass of falling ice and snow forced the displaced air up like a geyser. Everything grew quiet. Todd sobbed briefly and then stopped.

Direct rays of the late afternoon sun were blocked by the ten-thousand-foot ridge and higher peaks to the west. Juan's boots crunched on the crust of ice forming on the snow as the temperature dropped. He was trying to walk quietly to Roy. "Boss, this is heavy stuff. What is going on?"

"Wish I knew," Roy answered. "There are some traditional rivalries between different groups but this is a little more than that."

"Juan, a second ago when it was quiet did you hear anything strange?"

"Like?"

"Like a helicopter a long ways away. Maybe it was the wind."

They both listened to the stillness in the cold air.

"Yeah, just then, I heard it, or something." Juan looked to the northeast then back in the direction they had been traveling. "Long ways away."

"James," Roy's voice shattered the quiet, "Can you and Eugene start dinner? We'll set up camp here and call it a day. Tomorrow we should reach the Nunatak."

Roy caught Kurt's attention, nodded in the direction of a small knoll and walked slowly toward it. Kurt followed a few seconds later. "What were you suggesting?" Roy asked when they were out of sight of the others.

"Marcy has been in my tent for, what...four nights. She seems to be getting," he paused a second, "comfortable. Talks a lot, tells me things that are personal. What bothers me a little is she mentioned that she had a younger sister who was raped a year or so ago. It happened at a ski resort in Colorado. She thought it was somebody from Wallace Images so she applied for a job with the idea of tracking the person down. She had the credentials. She looked sort of strange a few minutes ago."

CHAPTER 6
REVENGE

Roy heard Kurt's voice calling him while Kurt shook the tent. "Roy, wake up. Marcy is missing."

"How can she be missing? What time is it?"

"She got up a while ago. Maybe one o'clock. She said she had to go to the bathroom. I went back to sleep."

"Okay, I'm getting up. It's two now. Go shake up Juan and check on Ian and Ralph." Roy unzipped his mummy bag and felt the cold air draw the heat away from the nylon liner inside. In a few seconds he had his pants on and slipped his feet into his boots. He slid his feet outside and sat inside the opening of the tent while he laced his boots.

Kurt came back and indicated that Ralph was not in the tent. "Ian said he had gone out to pee."

Juan and Ian came over. Roy grabbed his day-pack and a rope and the four of them jogged to the top of the knoll. It was two-fifteen in the morning. The evening sky was lit by a bright moon. The glacier was pale white. There were no shadows and crevasses seemed like gray voids. One hundred yards to the west it looked like someone sitting on the snow. It might have been a rock but there were no rocks on this part of the glacier. They walked roped up, as a precaution, and headed toward the object. As they got closer they could see that it was Ralph sitting in a belay position with the rope going up to a hole in the surface. It looked like someone had stepped into another hidden crevasse. Roy called to Ralph as they approached. Ralph did not move. Roy called to Marcy. There was no answer.

Ralph was in a sitting position. He faced the crevasse. His feet were spread apart to form a triangle. His ice axe was pushed into the snow down to the head and a prussic line anchored the rope that went into the crevasse to the ice axe. Ralph's right hand held the brake end of the rope. Another ice axe was plunged into his back.

Ian stopped and vomited. Juan moved him away from the spot and had him sit down. Roy checked Ralph for a possible pulse. He was dead. Kurt observed that the bleeding had stopped. The back of Ralph's parka was stained. In the moonlight the stain was black.

Kurt grabbed the adz of the axe and pulled the pick from the body.

"We will need this," he said as he pushed the shaft into the snow. He tied a prussic knot on the rope that went into the hole and anchored the rope

126

to the ice axe. "Help me move Ralph," he said to Roy. They pulled the body away from the hole in the glacier. A large stain in the snow marked where Ralph had died.

Kurt called for Marcy. There was no answer.

Roy took a harness out of his pack and asked Juan to belay him. While Juan kicked holes in the glacier's surface where he could brace his feet, Roy probed with his ice axe as he moved toward the hole in the snow. It was on the edge of the crevasse. He called into the black shadowless void, "Marcy!"

He heard a groan. "Juan, set up an anchor and lower me. I heard her down there. Kurt, set up a pulley system. Ian, follow the tracks back to camp to get the others. We need some muscle power to pull her out."

Juan said, "Okay, belay ready." when he was in position. Roy hacked a hole in the surface to make a second opening into the crevasse to the left of the one Marcy had fallen through. He placed his ice axe along the edge of the hole, lay down on his stomach, slid his feet into the void and lowered himself into crevasse. The rope ran over the top of the ice axe so as not to cut into the icy edge of the crevasse. He felt the rope jerking as Juan lowered him into the black abyss. He switched on his head lamp and called, "Marcy, do you hear me?" At twenty feet from the top he could see Marcy hanging limp in her harness against the smooth ice wall. She groaned.

"Help," she said weakly and seemed to try to get into a sitting position.

Roy pushed his feet against the wall of the crevasse and swung in her direction, then pendulumed back. He kicked again and developed enough momentum to reach her and grab her rope. He anchored it to his with a carabineer.

"Anything feel broken? Can you move?" He gently squeezed her arms and legs and pushed gently against her ribs and along her backbone. She winced briefly when he pushed against her waist. Falling twenty feet can result in severe bruises. The rope cutting into the edge of the crevasse as she fell appeared to absorb the heavy jolt of the sudden stop. She was able to talk quietly and indicated she wasn't hurt.

A rope slithered down into the void and brushed against Roy's head. He fastened it to Marcy's harness and told Juan to haul away. Marcy was lifted to the surface. When she saw Ralph's body she screamed and passed out.

In a matter of minutes the group pulled Roy to the surface.

"Whose ice axe is that?" Roy asked.

James answered. "I think it's Todd's."

"Where is Todd?" Roy asked. "Everybody else is here. Harry, was Todd in the tent when you got up?"

"Yes. He came over here with us a few minutes ago." Harry looked around. "I don't know where he is now."

"Did he leave the tent tonight?"

"He might have. I was dead tired. I mean, I was really tired and was sleeping pretty hard. If he left the tent I might not have heard him."

Roy asked Juan, James, Grant and Harry to back-track to camp and see if they could spot Todd.

Kurt was kneeling, holding Marcy's torso and head up and shaking her gently. "Marcy," he said, "Marcy, you are safe." He repeated several times. She opened her eyes and looked into his.

"Marcy," Roy repeated as he knelt next to her. He took her hands and warmed them in his. She did not have gloves on and her hands were stiff and cold. "What happened? Why were you out here with Ralph?"

She blinked a couple of times and shook her head slowly. "I don't know. I got up to go to the bathroom and something hit me in the head. The next thing I remember is hanging from a rope inside a crevasse. It was so dark I couldn't see any-thing. I tried to call." She closed her eyes for a few seconds. "What is wrong with Ralph? Why was he on the ground?"

"He is dead. Somebody killed him. Stabbed him with an ice axe. It looks like they tried to kill you, too." Roy put his gloves on her hands. "Did you hear or see anything before you were hit."

"No."

"Maybe the murderer thought you witnessed the act and tried to get rid of you, too." Roy stood. He and Kurt helped her stand.

"We got him," Juan yelled from the knoll near camp.

Eugene and Grant coiled the ropes and pulled the ice axes out of the glacier. Eugene asked, "What do we do with Ralph?"

Roy said, "Let's deal with him later. He's not going anywhere."

"I didn't kill Ralph," Todd said. "I never left my tent. Ask Harry. Anybody could have taken my ice axe."

Roy asked, "Harry, did he leave the tent?"

"I don't know. I was extremely tired and went to sleep. I didn't hear Todd move or anyone else."

"Why did you run away?" James asked.

"I didn't," Todd replied. "I just couldn't bear the sight of Ralph lying there. I needed a drink. I knew I would be blamed. I just had to get away for a few minutes. What is going on? I didn't kill him. It had to be somebody else." As he talked his voice grew stronger. "I didn't do it. One of you is a murderer."

"Harry," Roy said, "why don't you move your bag into Ian's tent. Todd, get into your tent and stay there until we figure out what to do. Juan, get Ralph's sleeping bag and other items from his tent before Todd gets in. Bring his belongings to my tent."

James asked, "What do we do with Ralph?"

"I guess we put him in his bag. We could tie him to the inside of the crevasse. That way," Roy suggested, "no predators can get to him until we get back to retrieve him."

Kurt, Roy, Eugene, James and Ian returned to the body. James and Eugene searched Ralph's pockets and put everything they found in a small sack. "Here," Roy said handing Eugene a small plastic case, "put this in one of his pockets."

"What is that?' Kurt asked.

"A small homing device," Roy answered, "we can find him from the air if the glacier gets covered with more snow."

Eugene asked, "How about Mr. Wallace?"

"I put one with his body." Roy responded.

"Does that mean that anyone can find them?" Kurt asked.

"Only if they have a transmitter and receiver at the right frequency," Roy answered, "These units can be found by some government agencies."

"Like who?" Eugene asked, "DEA? CIA?"

"You read too many spy stories," Roy said. "These are used by the Coast Guard and some Interior Department agencies for search and rescue operations. Primarily at sea."

"Was that a Coast Guard helicopter I heard this afternoon?" Eugene asked. "Were they picking up Mr. Wallace's body?"

"I don't believe so." Roy looked at Eugene. "When did you hear a helicopter? There was no distress signal given and no reason for them to be looking for us."

Eugene looked surprised. "I thought you all heard it. It was just after Michael fell in the crevasse."

Kurt and Roy put Ralph into the sleeping bag. Ian lowered the body. Eugene belayed Kurt and James belayed Roy as they went into the crevasse with the body. Kurt and Roy each put three ice screws into the wall of the crevasse and anchored the sleeping bag holding the body.

CHAPTER 7
NUNATAK

The mood in camp was somber during breakfast. Nobody mentioned Ralph. Todd stayed in his tent. Roy suggested to Juan that he take some food to Todd, then help him take down the tent. The general feeling was that Todd murdered Ralph and everybody wanted to keep their distance from him. The reality of the situation was that Todd had to move with the team and not become a liability and endanger others.

During breakfast Roy went through Ralph's belongings. His wallet had a drivers license, insurance card, two credit cards, plastic data cards, company ID card and a little over two hundred dollars. If he had a computer and a data card reader he might find out a little more about Ralph's past. The plastic bag had sunglasses, Swiss army knife and a small diary. Each night Ralph jotted a few notes about the trip. Roy reviewed the pages quickly.

July 9...Flew to Juneau then to Lituya Bay and helicopter to glacier feeding into Brady Glacier. Awesome, huge country. The members of the party are.... have Ian for tent mate.

July 10...Learning how to walk on glaciers... basic safety concepts. Learned how to climb out of a crevasse.

July 11...More basic techniques. Tiring. Kurt Rail looks familiar? Long tiring day. Storm moving in. Starting to snow heavily.

July 12...Lazy day.

July 13..Narrow escape last night-Ian and I trapped in tent by snowfall.... start trip westward, lots of avalanches. A long slog in soggy snow.

July 14..Mr. Wallace died accidentally last night. Hiked for four hours. Todd came unglued. He really needs a drink. Put in four more hours of trudging.

Kurt was rafting guide with Ron North (XYCore) in their trip last year! His picture is on Ron's desk at home...mentioned it to Tom. Big blowup.. Michael and Grant went at it again. Peggy got mentioned... will talk to Todd tomorrow.

Roy slipped the diary into his parka and put the other items back in the bag. "Juan," he called, "put this bag in your pack. It doesn't weigh too much."

Roy called Brad and gestured for him to come over.

"Brad," Roy started, "let's get out of hearing range of the others." They walked slowly east. "You know more about the staff than anyone because you checked them, approved their security reviews and so on and hear their petty grips. Right?"

"Yes."

Roy stopped and faced Brad. "Ralph has been murdered and Mr. Wallace was also murdered."

"No. Mr. Wallace's death was an accident."

"He was murdered. I won't go into how I know. Do you think Todd is the type who could kill someone?"

"He did find out Ralph was Peggy, his wife's, mystery man."

"Tell me, Brad, did he get angry? No. He was despondent. He almost seemed relieved. Do you think he would want to tell his wife he killed her lover? He doesn't seem to be the type."

"Maybe you are right," Brad said, "but then, if he didn't do it, who did? Who killed Mr. Wallace? Why?" He grabbed Roy's parka. "Who else will he kill?"

"I want to know everything possible about these people. All their skeletons," Roy asserted.

"There is confidential information," Brad said. He seemed shaken by Roy's request.

"Maybe you will be the next victim," Roy ventured.

"Okay, okay...where do you want to start?" Brad seemed broken. He was giving up the one thing he had prided himself on over the years. He could keep secrets. The others were more brilliant and had the technological insights. The others could design new products, build a factory, and produce products that were prized by the military and the largest corporations in the world. Brad listened, he soothed, and he did not betray confidences. The brilliant people needed him.

"Start by telling me about you. What is it you don't want others to know?"

Brad looked everywhere, at the sky, his feet, the distant Nunatak and finally at Roy. "I'm gay."

"Anything else?" Roy's response was matter of fact.

"No."

"Don't worry; you'll learn to live with it," Roy almost seemed to chide Brad but at the same time legitimized his personell preferences. "The question is, does anybody else know and does it place you at risk? Do you have any ...lovers at Wallace Images?"

"Grant."

"Grant is your lover?"

"Grant is bi..bisexual. When things get really tough for him, I help him. I stay with him. I love him."

"Christ," Roy muttered, "I'm sorry, I lost my focus for a second. Tell me," Roy regained a neutral, matter-of-fact voice, "does anybody else know about

Grant. Is your knowledge about him a threat to him, or to you?"

"Oh, God! I hope not."

"Relax. Is anyone at Wallace a threat to Grant?"

"He thinks Ian McGregor is after his job. I don't think Ian is. Grant seems to be in love with his big computer and has been paranoid about the smaller PC's that Ian keeps pushing. Some people think he has gone overboard in his relationship with his computer. Obsessive. Ian and others call him retread."

"Others?"

"Well, Ralph did, and other staff members and sometimes Harry and Michael when they were angry about something."

"How about James Wallace? Any issues?"

"He is, ah... was, always fighting with Raymond, Mr. Wallace, his brother, about the best way to run the company. I think he didn't like the pedestal his brother put Michael Kirby on. But, I don't think he has any skeletons. He is just trying to come out from under his brother's shadow."

Brad looked at Roy in a panic. "I don't even know how to talk about Mr. Wallace any more. Is...was...I can't believe he isn't here any more; and Ralph not here."

"Harry Kuznets, Director of Finance. Does he have any weak spots?"

Brad said, "I don't know if I can do this. There are things that are best forgotten."

"Like, Marcy's sister was raped by Ralph. That was best forgotten, right? What is it you don't want to tell me about Harry?"

"What are you saying about Ralph and Marcy?" Brad quizzed.

"Let's come back to it later. What about Harry?"

"Harry had... had a drug problem. It started five or six years ago. Two years ago I got him into a treatment program in Colorado for ten weeks. Everybody else thought he supposedly was taking care of his mother. Nobody else knows but me. He hasn't had any problems since he got back."

"Are you sure?"

"Yes. We are friends. Not lovers, if that is what you mean. He knows I helped him with his problem and haven't betrayed him. Until now."

"Don't worry."

"Boss," Juan said as he came over the rise on the glacier that blocked the view of camp.

"Juan, go back. Keep everyone in camp. Make coffee or something until we come back." Roy waved Juan away.

"Don't worry about Juan. He has worked for me for ten years. I'll stake my life and yours on him."

"What do you know about Marcy? When did she join Wallace Images?"

Brad responded with a question. "What was it you said about Ralph and her sister? I didn't know she had a sister."

"Does she have a family?

"No. Very tragic life." Brad stopped and took a big breath. "Her parents were killed in a car wreck when she was thirteen. She didn't have any brothers or sisters. Her aunt and uncle in Golden Colorado put her through school. She majored in accounting and worked for several large accounting firms. Mostly institutional accounting."

"Did you check her out personally, verify her application and all that, or did a government agency do the security check?"

"No, I didn't validate her application. Harry said he did and vouched for her. Now that you ask, she didn't have a security check because she wasn't working on any restricted projects."

"Did Harry know her before she applied?"

"I don't think so."

"Tell me about Tom."

"Dr. Gilmore is a brilliant electrical engineer. MIT graduate. Most of the products Wallace Images is famous for he created. The company should be called Gilmore Images. Tom and Mr. Wallace seemed to find each other. Mr. Wallace was good at selling ideas and knew government procurement. He was retired from the Air Force in contracting. Tom was interested in creating, so he created and Mr. Wallace sold."

"How does Tom get along with Michael Kirby?"

"They hate each other. I think it is more than a difference in professional opinion. Tom acts like Michael is ripping at his insides."

"So tell me about Michael. We can come back to Tom."

"Michael was hired by James about four years ago to help Wallace Images develop a capability to produce their products. Some think it was really Mr. Wallace's idea. Up until then Tom and his staff would design, develop and demonstrate a new product. The product was then actually produced and distributed by an associated subsidiary. James thought Wallace Images could increase its profits if it also produced, so they hired Michael to be in charge of engineering, which is really manufacturing. His background was engineering. They sent him to MIT for a summer program to study manufacturing management. Mr. Wallace thought vertical integration provided better control over ideas as well as profits."

"How about Michael and Ray Wallace. You said James hired him."

"James did hire him. Michael knew that Mr. Wallace was the person in charge and told him everything he was doing. Michael was able to get Mr. Wallace to approve of his ideas and sign the spending authorizations, even when Harry in

Finance or Tom didn't like the idea. Mr. Wallace seemed to like him. Somehow Michael avoided the battle between James and Mr. Wallace."

"How about Eugene?"

Brad started to answer. "A spook..." when Juan came over the rise a second time.

"I'm sorry, boss, but every body is getting antsy. I think we gotta go."

Roy looked at Brad. "We will talk later. Thanks."

"Nunatak means 'rock in the snow'." Roy pointed to the distinct feature to the west. It rose three hundred feet and looked like a small mountain that pushed a sharp head up from the glacier. The top hundred feet was dark rock. Below the rock was a shelf about the size of a basketball court that dropped off to the glacier below. The south and west sides of the Nunatak tapered and blended in with the glacier. The slope grew steeper from south to east to the north side. The north side was a two-hundred-foot rock cliff. The east side was a vertical ice cliff that blended in with the rock face on the north. Around the base of the north and northeast side was a bergshrund, a void caused by the ice pulling away from the rock.

The glacial ice north of the Nunatak was over one thousand feet thick. The glacier was moving from west to southeast. As the glacier flowed past the Nunatak the ice pulled away from the rock on the east side and left a chasm two hundred feet deep.

"A geological characteristic of that Nunatak is its mineral composition. It assayed over 90 percent iron and nickel ore. There were large, car-sized pods of nearly pure ore."

"You can tell all that from over here," James said, "amazing."

"No, not from here. Somewhere in my past I spent two years up here working as a mountain climber for an exploration mining company. There was a small team of us. We sampled rocks on the moraines and climbed up cliffs to get samples. We also spent a lot time surveying and using geophysical devices to measure the extent of the mineral deposits under the glacier in the area. Doodle bugging it was called."

"How do you measure mineral deposits under the glacier?" Tom asked.

"Let's talk about that later. We have to get started. It doesn't look that far to the Nunatak but we won't be able to travel in a straight line. There are crevasses between here and there you could drop a battleship into.

CHAPTER 8
RESCUE

The Nunatak loomed in front of the group like a mirage. After five hours of searching for a solid path through the maze of crevasses and thin snow bridges the Nunatak seemed as far away as it did when they started. Crevasses that were to wide to step over had to be circumvented by walking around one end or the other.

When there was a snow bridge it had to be tested to see if it would hold the heaviest person. This meant that Harry was the guinea pig. If it held him it would hold the others. Usually Roy or Kurt could judge if the bridge would hold Harry's weight.

The first time a bridge had to be tested Harry swore he would go on a diet. He wasn't enthusiastic about going where no man had gone before. He would leave his pack on the ground and pull it over after he crossed. He did not want to fall into a crevasse carrying his pack. He probed with his ice axe in his right hand, right foot forward. He probed a few inches, moved his right foot a few inches, then shuffled his left foot up to his right foot. Each time he probed he looked back at Kurt who was belaying, then tugged on the rope gently trying to reassure himself that he was secure.

Once he crossed the bridge he would belay the next person. The last person on a rope would use a half-length of rope to belay the first person on the next rope team.

Coordinating the crossing of each team took extra time. Tenuous snow bridges were crossed only when the distance around the crevasse was great.

Harry was five feet out on the third bridge that he tested when it collapsed. Kurt was quick in pulling in the slack that was in the line, but Harry still fell in six feet. The rope cut back into the remainder of the bridge so much that Harry was under the lip and out of sight. The rope that Kurt held seemed to go straight into the glacier surface.

Juan belayed while Roy went over the edge of the crevasse next to the collapsed bridge. He threw Harry a second rope. Harry tied to it. Kurt slowly let out rope and Harry dropped further into the crevasse but out from under the bridge. Ian, Mike, and Brad were able to pull him up out of the crevasse without having to bother with prussic and bulgari knots. Everybody in the group cheered when Harry stood up and put his pack on. He felt relieved to be on top and relaxed knowing that if he did fall in he could easily be rescued.

Roy was at the head of the first rope as they started their trek around the crevasse. At times he walked at a leisurely pace. Other times he would say to Grant, second on his rope, "Give me a belay." He would slow down or stop and probe gingerly at the surface in front of him. Nothing perceptible was different to Grant about the surface. Roy would say, "Okay," and they would continue. The third time Roy asked for a belay he pushed his ice axe into the snow. A gaping hole appeared as a four-square-foot section of the surface fell into a hidden crevasse. Roy backed up and detoured around what he judged to be the crevasse, probing all the way.

The next time Roy uncovered a hidden crevasse Harry asked, "How do you do that?"

"Do what?"

"Know there is a crevasse there."

"Worms. Sound."

Harry repeated Roy's answer but as a question, "Worms? Sound? What are you talking about?"

"I'll tell you when we take a stop for lunch." Roy continued probing.

It was mid afternoon before a collective chorus of, "Lets take a break," was heard. Roy said, "Ah, teamwork!"

The first team stopped and the first person coiled up the rope as the next person slowly approached. Everyone stood until the last person arrived. Roy sensed a tension in the group. Todd dropped his pack and sat down. "I'm beat," he said. The others moved away slightly and dropped their packs. Roy placed his pack next to Todd's.

"Has anybody noticed the warm front moving in from the south?" Roy pointed to the south. The glacier was more than twenty-five miles long to the south and ten miles wide. A flat gray mass of clouds sloping thirty-five degrees dropped onto the southern horizon of the glacier. The sky was still clear and blue due east and to the north. The sloped wedge of cloud was moving slowly north. The southern end of the glacier was gone from sight.

"That looks like nasty weather headed our way," James commented. "When will it get here?"

Roy watched the front and pointed to the high wispy cirrus clouds at the northern edge of the front. "Five, maybe six hours. We should make it to the base of the Nunatak and have a chance to make camp before it hits. But we have to keep moving."

Conversations stopped as exhaustion set in after sitting for a few minutes. Juan beckoned James and Marcy inviting them to help him prepare lunch. Stoves were lit, water boiled and some coffee and cocoa made. Everyone munched on cheese, some sausage and Trisket crackers. Lunch was not fancy.

Swirling winds at the leading edge of the storm carried a distant sound. During the lull in conversation the sound of a helicopter drifted in on the breeze from the east. For the last couple of days the faint sounds of a helicopter could be heard near evening moving to the south. Now it seemed to be moving north, possibly cut off from the south by the storm.

"Who do you think that is boss?" Juan asked.

"Don't know. Might be a prospector or National Park Rangers. It would be nice if they came by and we could let them know what has happened." Roy wondered if he really wanted outside people in just yet. He wasn't convinced that Todd had killed Ralph. The reasons for the deaths of Raymond Wallace and Ralph were unexplained. A helicopter arriving could possibly give the murderer a chance to escape.

The lunch break was over. One by one the group stood, put on their packs and clipped their waist carabiners onto the rope. The sun was midway down its climb from the sky. The sun's rays were at a low angle after they passed over Mt. LaPerouse and highlighted the cliffs of the northeastern boundary of the glacier fifteen miles away. The sound of the helicopter came and went with the wind. Somewhere in the faint cycle of sound there was a harsh sputter, an irregular grating of sound, a hint of metal striking rock. The sound stopped. Everybody listened.

Eugene said, "I bet that chopper crashed."

"We had better get moving," Roy said. "That storm won't wait for us. If there is a problem over there, there is not much we can do from here."

There was a new sense of urgency about traveling, surviving and being prepared. The pace picked up but was tempered by the circumstances of the surrounding environment.

"You know," Harry called to Roy, "you didn't explain the worms and sounds bit."

"Okay," Roy said, "have you noticed the sound of your feet on the snow?"

"No."

"Listen and watch. It has been several days since it snowed. The sun has been hot and the nights cold. During the day the snow melts and at night it freezes. Each time there is melting and freezing, ice crystals form and get larger."

"I'm with you so far. Not exactly rocket science."

"Now, can you see that you are stepping on a thin crusty layer of granulated ice crystals in contrast to the soft snow of two to three days ago?"

"Yeah, now that you mention it."

"Now that you are focused on it, can you hear the sound of the ice crystals when you scuff your feet on them."

"You are right."

"Now comes the tricky part. Advanced thermo-dynamics. If there is a hidden crevasse, the temperature under the snow surface is different than where the glacier is solid. You might not be able to measure that difference but it is there and it influences the way the ice crystals form. I think the term used to talk about the formation of the ice is *nevation*. Anyway, if you spend enough time out here your subconscious will start picking up on the subtle changes in sound and will tell you that there might be a hidden crevasse."

"Okay, what about the worms?"

"My dear Dr. Watson," Roy, chided Harry "we are looking at a biological extension of the thermal differential hypothesis."

"Which means?"

"Have you noticed that there all kinds of little critters on the snow and ice? See, there is a spider." Roy pointed to a small spider that has blown in on the wind. "There are all kinds of things that blow in on the wind or are dropped by birds. Also, there is an annelid, a worm that is common in the Pacific Northwest, Alaska and Greenland called a snow worm. Scoop a handful of snow and watch it for awhile."

They walked a distance with Harry studying the chunk of snow and ice. "I'll be damned. There is something here, thinner than a human hair, black and about three-eighths of an inch long. It is crawling."

"Right, a worm. The number of snow worms in a square meter is influenced by the temperature of the ice. Again, hidden crevasses influence the number of worms because of the temperature of air flowing under the ceiling of the crevasse."

"You can detect that?"

"I like to tell people I can. I really don't know for sure but I do find the crevasses. Shit! Belay on."

Roy's left foot stepped into a void and he threw his weight backwards. His right hip and pack landed on solid ice and left leg hung over a crevasse. "Pull hard on the rope!" he yelled to Harry.

Harry pulled and Roy squirmed back onto solid surface. Standing he probed for the boundary and direction of the crevasse with his ice ax.

"Sometimes it is hard to observe with the subconscious when the mouth is open," Roy said. "Ancient proverb."

"Okay everybody, fun is over. Let's get going," Roy yelled back to the teams that had stopped.

"Another subtlety of the surface," Roy continued, "there is algae growing on the surface that adds a reddish color to the ice. The growth of the algae is influenced by temperature gradients. There will be a quiz. Up here and on Greenland there is a form of snow flea. I don't use them to find crevasses."

"Hey, Roy," Tom called from farther back in the line of ropes, "there is a signal coming from the rocks on the other side of the glacier."

A reflection flashed from the area where the helicopter sounds were last heard. The gray bank of clouds had almost reached the cliffs. Everything to the south was obscured. The flash of reflected sunlight was regular. Three fast flashes, three longer flashes, three shorter flashes. "S-O-S." The signal repeated.

James said, "What can we do?"

"Nothing right now," Roy responded, "except hustle our butts and get to where we can make camp.

Another hour should it." Roy opened his parka, pulled out a compass hanging from a cord around his neck and took a sighting on the direction of the flashes."

A few minutes later the slanted storm moved north and the cliffs disappeared from sight.

CHAPTER 9
FOG

The light grew dim as the clouds lowered. Roy probed as fast as he could with his right arm, stabbing at the ice in front of him with his ice ax, and taking a step. He wanted to go faster but he had to be able to stop his forward motion if the ice axe broke through the surface.

The glacier seemed more stable the last mile before the Nunatak. It was like a quiet eddy in the frozen river. Visibility deteriorated as the storm clouds reached down to the glacier surface. He could no longer see Kurt and Ian on the last rope.

The flat surface of the glacier started to slope upward. It was impossible to see the Nunatak but Roy had been going in the same direction according to the compass for the past half-hour. He figured they were approaching the base of the Nunatak and could make camp. They would have to wait until tomorrow to search for the supply drop. Roy stopped and coiled up the rope as Michael walked toward him. Over the next few minutes the other rope teams arrived.

"Set up the tents in a circle with the openings facing the center," Roy said when everyone had unclipped from their ropes and dropped their packs. "Juan, run a hundred-foot line out, in that direction, north, and anchor it to this ice axe." Roy walked out past what would be the perimeter of the circle of tents and pushed an ice axe into the snow.

"Hello, everyone," he talked loud enough so that everyone could hear, "the pot of gold and the latrine are at the other end of the line that Juan is setting up. Use the line as a handrail when you need to tend to business. I don't want anybody wandering off in the storm and getting lost. The visibility is down to fifty feet and might get worse."

"Michael, Todd and Brad, you are the chefs for the evening. Grant and Ian, will you set up the cooking tent before you set up your own tents?"

Marcy came over to Roy and said, "I am feeling funny about last night. Would it create a problem if I slept alone tonight? I mean, can you arrange it with Kurt. I really want to gather my thoughts and stretch out. Nothing against Kurt, it's just that when I feel stressed I like to be alone."

"No problem. I want to work with Juan on something tonight anyway, which will free up Tom's tent. I'll move Kurt in with Tom. How are you doing?"

"I'm beat," she said. "We really pushed hard today and last night didn't help. Did Todd kill Ralph?"

"I really don't know," he answered after a few seconds. He didn't think Todd could have. But Marcy appeared to have motive. She could have killed Ralph and lowered herself into the crevasse knowing that someone would come along.

Roy talked to Tom and Kurt and suggested they share a tent for the night. They looked at each other and indicated they didn't have any problems with the arrangement. Kurt said he understood Marcy's wish for a quiet night. Roy also suggested that he and Kurt might make a forced march to the area where the signals came from.

"Hey, Boss," Juan called, "there is a problem in the kitchen."

Roy looked over toward where the cook tent was to be set up. Todd and Brad were standing off to the side. Roy heard Grant yell at Michael, "If you want to do it, go ahead."

Ian was pushing himself between Grant and Michael. "Come on, guys, cool it. We have to work together."

Grant looked at Ian and told him, "Butt out."

Roy walked over to the tent which was spread out on the snow. The stoves and cooking utensils were lying in the snow. He first encountered Todd and Brad. "What is the problem?"

Brad responded, "Michael is being a prick. He called everyone incompetent and said he was he going to show Ian and Grant how to set up the tent. Grant told him to shove the tent poles where they would do some good. Todd and I decided to get out of the way. If Michael wants to do everything, let him. Ian is trying to mediate, just like at the office. If Michael gets assertive it is best to get out of the way and wait."

"Michael," Roy said, walking to the stoves, "I thought you were cooking. Isn't it kind of hard to start a stove with a tent pole? Let them put up the tent. You, Todd and Brad, get the stoves, water and dinner going. We are running out of time."

By then everyone was watching to see what would happen.

Michael started to glare at Roy. For the first time that he could remember he noticed Roy's eyes, intensely dark brown with flecks of gold, that seemed capable of seeing into one's mind. Michael took a deep breath, grimaced, looked down at the snow and threw down the poles. "You're right."

"What are we having?" Roy asked.

"Mystery meal," Brad said, "I will read the ingredients and whoever guesses gets the first serving. Okay?"

James said, "Okay, I will play your silly game."

"Pasta made from durum semolina flour; Sour cream powder made from cream cultures, lactic acid, nonfat milk solids and citric acid. Cooked freeze-dried diced beef; Potato starch; Whey powder; Parmesan cheese powder made from milk, cheese cultures, enzymes and salt; Dehydrated mushrooms; Dehydrated tomato flakes; Butter buds made from whey solids, corn syrup solids, modified butter oil, dehydrated butter, salt, guar gum, annatto and turmeric and vegetable colors."

"Is that it?" James asked.

"No, there is more, I just ran out of breath. *It also includes onion granules, sea salt, nonfat dry milk, garlic granules, dehydrated green onions and spices.* Okay, what is it?"

"You know, Brad, I'm so hungry I'll eat it anyway," Marcy quipped.

"I know what it is," Juan said raising his hand.

Brad shook his head, "Staff, relatives and members of the manufacturing company and their families are not allowed to participate."

"Beef, noodles and cream. It must be Beef Stroganoff," Todd said to James.

"Beef Stroganoff," James said.

"And the winner is... the boss," Brad said holding up several packets of dehydrated Beef Stroganoff.

During dinner the rain started as a heavy mist, then turned into fine drops. The stoves were secured and everyone took their plates and cups to their tents.

The drops turned into a heavy rain. A few minutes later the wind picked up and buffeted the tents. The wind would push hard against the rain covers forcing them against the surface of the tents. A wet spot would appear where the two surfaces met. The wind would push and hold the two surfaces together for a few seconds and then slack off. From time to time the wind stopped completely and the air would be quiet. Then with the sound of an explosion the wind would slap the outer rain cover up against the tent wall hard enough to send the moisture collecting on the fabric wall flying across the inside of the tent.

Roy had Juan move into his tent. Roy estimated that the supply drop was either somewhere below the Nunatak near where they were at present or up on the small plateau at the base of the rock. There was food and there should be a radio that Juan could use to call George Baker. George could contact the police and National Park authorities and arrange to pick up the bodies. When the weather cleared enough to see, Juan would try to find the air-dropped supplies while Roy and Kurt tried to locate the helicopter crew.

"How come you can't contact the General?" Juan asked.

"We have some prearranged times and I haven't been able to get isolated enough to discuss things without being noticed."

During the night the rain turned to snow. Every half-hour or so one or two people would be out clearing their tents. If they saw a tent getting covered too deeply they might brush it off or call to those inside to clear the tent.

Roy was out clearing his tent and could hear Tom and Kurt in a muffled conversation. "I can't do that," Tom said in an agitated voice.

"You have to," Kurt said. Tom got out of the tent. He pushed the snow off the top and away from the sides.

When the snow stopped, everybody relaxed enough to sleep soundly.

"Boss," Juan said as he poked his head outside the tent, "something strange out here. The ice axes are buzzing." He got out of the tent and followed the line to the latrine area. As he walked he had to pull the line out of the snow. The snow had covered it. No one else had been out yet.

Roy looked out at the wet fog shrouding the tents and obliterating the view of the glacier. It was 5:30 and the early morning light was dull. He couldn't see more than forty feet and the fog blended in with the fresh snow.

Eugene crawled out of his tent. "Whoa! My buttons are dancing." Condensed moisture on the metal snaps on his parka was dancing in little droplets. "My hair is standing on end. What's going on?"

Roy laughed a little and said, "Static electricity. Wait until you try to pee. Your pubic hair will stand on end. A very strange feeling."

"This is rare but it happens. We are in the middle of an electrical cloud. Sooner or later the cloud will discharge. Bolts of lightning and all that."

"Let's move all the iron objects away from the tents. They might act as the point of discharge."

Juan came back. "Hey, boss. That was weird, my hair down there, you know what I mean, it tickled."

"Okay, everybody," Roy shouted loudly enough for everybody to hear, "we are in the middle of an electrical cloud." He waited a few seconds. One head after another popped out of tents. "Move your hardware, ice axes, crampons, carabiners, stoves and pans away from the tents, to the area where Juan is standing. To be safe, move your pack frames. We will cook breakfast after it clears."

"Juan, scatter the stuff around a bit. We don't want all the ice axes fused together."

James asked, "How long will this thing last?

"The last one I was in lasted a full day. It interrupted all radio transmissions and reception. It discharged to a rock outcrop near our camp and the radio interference ended immediately. We just sit it out."

Roy took all the items out of his big backpack and moved it out the area where equipment was scattered. He put it down and surveyed the other items. Eugene's pack was lying on his ice axe. Roy picked it up to move it and noticed its weight. He glanced quickly to see if Eugene was in sight. Not seeing Eugene he reached into the pack and felt the cold metallic shape of a 45 automatic. He moved the pack away from the ice axe and returned to the tent area.

"We are not going to be doing much until this cloud goes away. You might as well go back to sleep."

"Juan, we have to wait for this to clear before Kurt and I will go across the glacier and see if we can find out what happened to the chopper we heard and who sent the signal. In the meantime we will wait for the big flash."

"I can remember some great lightning storms in Mazatlan," Juan said. "You could see the lightning going from the clouds down to the water on the horizon, out past the bay. The lightning clouds would come, moving in toward shore. The lightning followed.

When it first started you could see the lightning but no sound. When it came closer the sound grew louder but the sound took a long time to be heard. The closer the storm got the louder the thunder was, and the time it took to be heard got shorter. When the storm got real close the sound came at the same time as the flash of light. That was scary."

James crouched in front of Roy's tent. "It looks like we might have time to kill. Michael and I were wondering about your doodle bugging, I think you called it."

Roy went over to James and Michael's tent. "Cozy in here. What did you want to know."

"We create images from telemetry data." Michael began., "You it seems were involved in finding mineral deposits under a thousand feet of ice. Basically mapping out something that couldn't be seen. We are starting some new projects that involve creating images of unseen things. We like to get ideas from other fields of study. It helps to think differently. You had mentioned mineral mapping to Harry and we got curious. How did you do it?"

"What are your projects?" Roy asked.

"It is too early to discuss anything in detail, mind you." James approached Roy's question cautiously.

"One is a model of the migration of tectonic plates over time."

"Over what period of time?"

"Whatever time frame is needed." James glanced at Michael. "Some researchers are thinking about forever. Since the continents split off from Pangea, the super continent. Don't ask us who."

"Fair enough," Roy responded, "we used two methods for locating mineral deposits and then drilled through the ice and obtained core samples for verification. One method was to set up a transmitter, a radio station with a very boring program and a person with a receiver running around on the glacier trying to find the program.

"The transmitter was a gasoline driven power source and an antenna that looked like the outline of a sailboat. There was a mast twelve feet high and a boom twelve feet wide. The antenna wires looped around the ends of the boom and the top of the mast. The signal was directional and was positioned by rotating the boom. The person with the receiver ran in the direction the boom pointed and recorded the time difference between the air signal and the ground signal."

"What do you mean, air signal and ground signal?" Michael asked.

"The signal from the transmitter is an electromagnetic radio signal. It moves at one speed in the air. The signal is also transmitted though the minerals in the ground. The higher the mineral content of the ground, the faster the signal travels.

The receiver in the field would measure the difference in time for the signal to arrive between the air and ground. The larger the time differences the higher the potential mineral content. There were many of variables including type of mineral, dispersion, and depth. Not a real exact measurement but enough to give the geophysicists and geologists a clue as to where they wanted to drill and get core samples."

"Sounds like a lot of leg work," Michael said.

"You are right. The geologists marked a grid pattern on a map with the width of the grid being 1000 yards. The transmitter would be moved to each intersection on the grid and the receiver would be run along the grid lines. That was on the glacier. In some areas we set the transmitter on the top of a ridge. A helicopter moved the transmitter operator around to different locations, dropping him off and moving away to avoid interfering with the transmitter signal. In those days all the data was recorded by hand and the data points were plotted by hand. The geologists were very busy at night. Nowadays data loggers record the data and the data is uploaded to a computer for plotting."

"What was the other method?" James asked.

"An Audio Frequency Magnetometer," Roy said, "which was used to measure the pattern of the earth's magnetic field. The basic idea is that if bipolar molecules are oriented, lined up, in a temporary magnetic field and the temporary magnetic field is released, the rate at which they return to normal random motion is influenced by the field they are in. So," Roy asked, "what is the field they are left in?"

Michael looked at James, then Roy and said, "I guess it is the earth's magnetic field."

"Correct," Roy nodded. "We had a device that contained a liter of deuterium, heavy water; a battery for exciting an electromagnet and instruments that would pick up the signal given off by the deuterium molecules when they lined up with the earth's magnetic field.

"The water bottle was mounted on a swivel on a pack frame. The orientation and dip in the earth's field could be measured by orienting the bottle horizontally and vertically until a maximum reading was obtained. The geologists also plotted this data every night. The orientation of the field and the dip are influenced by type of mineral and mineral concentration."

"Wow," Michael uttered looking at James. "Do you know what kind of signal was being given off?"

"No."

"Not a hell of a lot of-what, is it called.?" . . he talked to himself, "a Bohr Magnetron. The amount of energy released when a molecule drops from one energy state to a lower one."

"Remember," Roy interjected, "there are a lot of molecules in the bottle so the combined signal is measurable."

"Right," Michael said, "with both techniques you are looking for ways in which minerals influence electromagnetic characteristics of the earth. But there are no direct measures."

"You're right." Roy said as he stretched and turned to sit at the opening of the tent to leave. "No direct measures, but clues as to where to use direct methods, like drilling."

"Thanks." James said as Roy left the tent.

Roy could hear Michael as he walked back to his own tent. "James, have we tried reorienting our new hologram projections by resetting the holo-object magnetic control properties?"

"Didn't know they had a magnetic control feature," James responded. "It makes sense. We have to give it try. Michael, why don't you suggest the idea to Tom? I doubt he would consider it if it came from me."

The moisture on Roy's parka buttons buzzed and drops of moisture that collected on them shimmered and danced as he headed for his tent. More electromagnetic stuff, he thought.

Just before 11:00 AM the fog exploded in a bright flash at the same time that the sound hissed. The first sound was the hissing crackle of electricity being discharged. The air along the path of arc heated and expanded creating a vacuum. Air rushing into the void from all directions collided. The hiss and explosion were deafening. The flash and sound happened simultaneously. The lightning discharged somewhere between the tents and the top of the Nunatak.

The sound was disorienting. The concussion of the explosion knocked Roy's breath away.

"We're dea.." Juan started to say, when a second explosion followed immediately by a third. There was a heavy aroma of ozone.

"Is it over?" Juan asked a few seconds after the third explosion.

"I think so. Look outside."

Juan poked his head out of the tent. The static was gone and the air was clearing. Heads poked out from all of the tents.

"I hope that didn't hit our food supply," Juan said as he climbed out of the tent and stood in the fresh snow. "The buzz is gone."

CHAPTER 10
CHOPPER

Kurt was first on the rope, pushing through the snow at a steady pace faster than a walk but not quite running. Roy followed fifty feet back. Even though the fresh snow was only eight inches to twelve inches deep, the trough created by the Kurt made it easier for Roy to move.

The fresh snow obscured the subtle hints of the treacherous hidden crevasses. The large crevasses were wide open and easy to see. For the first hour they retraced their route of the previous day, skirting around the southern end of the large crevasse field formed by the slow-motion turbulence of two large glaciers merging. For the next three hours they moved due north following the center of the large glacier. Every forty-five minutes they switched the lead position.

The sky grew clearer as the day passed. The electrical cloud of the morning had acted like a magnet holding the fog close to the glacier. When the charge dissipated, the fog started lifting. After the third hour of travel the view to the north was unobstructed. By the fourth hour the Nunatak, where the rest of the party remained, was barely visible.

Roy started a mental calculation of where the signals had come from. The compass bearing was 13 degrees, a little east of north, when the clouds had moved in the day before. Now he wanted to determine where the path they were following would intersect an imaginary line 13 degrees from the Nunatak.

He set the targeting bezel on his compass to 193 degrees and kept the compass oriented north. When the targeting bezel finally pointed back to the Nunatak he knew they had found the place where they had to change direction.

"Kurt, bear off to your right and head for the midpoint on the north ridge of that peak. Do you see that outcropping that looks like two types of rock, one granite, the other basalt. Head for it."

"Okay," Kurt responded as he turned right.

Neither of them had slowed down while the course correction was computed and executed. Roy thought about how good it felt to be moving, steadily and fast for long periods of time. Like climbing long, steep snow slopes, breathing is deep and regular and rhythmic. He had often imagined it was a form of dynamic yoga. In this type of exertion he knew that the pace was determined by breathing. If the hill gets steeper the breathing stays at the same rate, but the step shortens.

If the slope gets so steep that the length of the step cannot be shortened, then slow down the pace. The trick to long distance and high altitude climbing is constant oxygen intake.

"If you try to go too fast you run out of oxygen." How many times had he said that over the years to climbing students? "If it is steep and you are at high altitude you might have to take two or three deep breaths between each step. Whatever you do, you have to get a rhythm. You have to put your muscles and balance on automatic pilot. Your mind just tags along with the body and absorbs what is passing by," he continued to muse.

"You know," he had often said, "you can even fall asleep and keep walking as in a trance. If you slip, you have to get your breathing going first, then move your legs into the rhythm."

"Until you can control your body by breathing, mountain climbing can be pure hell," he spoke aloud to himself.

"What did you say?" Kurt yelled back.

"Nothing. I was just talking to myself." Roy answered, realizing that he was vocalizing his thoughts. "It helps clean out your lungs, you know."

On his solo trip across Greenland he often found himself talking and shouting to groups of people. He liked to relive lectures and confrontations and romantic moments, but saying what he wished he had said rather than what he actually spoken.

Kurt had stopped at the edge of a deep bergschrund, a deep chasm between the snow and the rock cliff in front of them. He pulled in the rope as Roy walked up to him, keeping the same pace. Roy could hear that Kurt was breathing heavily, steadily, comfortably. They had just pushed eighteen miles without stopping. The last mile had gained two thousand feet of altitude and the slope they were now on was fifty degrees.

"How you doing?" Kurt asked. Roy glanced up. Kurt looked like a guide bringing a client up a steep cliff, confident, in control, in his element.

"Great. Really good. You?"

"Fine." Kurt turned and looked up at the rock buttress in front of them. There were cliffs on both sides of the buttress. It looked as if the cliff in front of them went up to another steep snow slope that ran into another cliff.

When they were still on the flatter glacier, a distance from the cliff, it looked like there was a piece of yellow metal jutting out of the serac on the slope above the cliff in front of them.

They both shouted up the cliff. "Is anybody up there? Hello?" There wasn't even an echo.

Roy shook his head as he looked at the cliff. "That is going to be tricky. Shall we flip a coin to see who climbs it?"

"No," Kurt said, "I'll do it."

"Alright, but we will have to wait until morning light. It is almost dark. Let's drop down to a flat area and bivouac."

A breeze was picking up, coming in from the south. The sun had set behind LaPerouse to the west sending red rays through the clouds that formed as the moist air blowing in from the Pacific Ocean was forced up to fourteen thousand feet.

"I can handle this." Kurt's voice had a slight sense of urgency. "If it gets too dark we can retreat and try again in the morning. Besides, if there is somebody up there, the difference between now and in the morning might save them."

"Okay, let me get anchored so I can belay you. It looks like you are going to have to drop into the serac and swing over to the face." Roy opened his pack and took out some pitons, a couple of friends, stoppers and bongs. "Here is some additional hardware. When you get there, see if their radio works. The batteries are probably dead, but give it a shot. See if you can get the serial number off the registration plate on the instrument console."

"Good, I have a couple of pitons. These could be useful." Kurt attached the items Roy handed him to the sling he draped over his shoulder. "I'll see what I can find."

The cliff was seventy feet high. The rock was granite. A couple of large cracks ran diagonally upwards from right to left. Near the top there was a slight bulge outward. On the right side of the buttress there was a boundary between the granite and a reddish basalt rock. The granite had been covered with volcanic basalt sometime in the past million years. Both tilted upward as the mountains were pushed up by the collision of the Pacific plate and the North American plate. The expansion of the Pacific trench forced the mass under the Pacific Ocean to push eastward and rotate clockwise. When the Pacific plate hits the North American plate it slides under it and forces the coastal land mass to rise, creating a mountain range and earthquakes.

Roy put an ice axe across the lip of the serac. Kurt lowered himself into the serac with the rope running over the ice axe. Roy let out twenty feet of rope before Kurt could swing over and get his feet on the rock. It took ten minutes for him to climb up above the lip of the serac. Once he was ten feet higher than Roy he placed a piton in a crack and drove it in with a hammer.

"Love that sound," Roy said. A piton going into a good crack has a bell-like ring to it as it is driven in. Once it is in, the sound is solid.

Kurt methodically worked his way up the cliff. This was not solid rock and every crack and hand-hold had to be tested.

Every ten to fifteen feet he put in a piton. The wedging action of one piton forced a small ledge to break away from the cliff. It fell three feet to the left of Roy and into the serac. The sound of the rocks falling into the void suggested that the serac was over a hundred feet deep.

It was nearly dark when Kurt disappeared over the bulge. He still had a short distance to climb.

"I'm here." Roy could barely hear Kurt yelling down. Kurt pounded on the metal frame of the helicopter with his hammer letting Roy know he had found it. Roy thought that Kurt would be a few minutes exploring the wreckage and checking for life signs. Since Kurt was on top Roy no longer had to tend to the belay. "Now I can make a call." He talked aloud to himself. "It has been four days since I have been by myself." He took the small communicator from his parka and pointed it in the direction of the satellite.

"Trigger to Gabby. Trigger to Gabby. Do you copy."

A response came back almost immediately. "Hello, Trigger. Get lost?"

"Gabby, lots of problems here. Two murders.. Raymond Wallace and Ralph Dresner.."

"Say again."

"Two murders.. Raymond Wallace and Ralph Dresner. One suspect but not certain. I need you to check on background of Ralph Dresner. Check history of company named XYCore and Ron North. Check history of Marcy Wallingford. Check history of Kurt Rail, my guide. Check history of Eugene Langley...possible CIA."

"Let me validate." The voice at the other end said. "Background on Ralph Dresner. History of XYCore and Ron North. Background on Marcy Wallingford. Background on Kurt Rail. Background on Eugene Langley. Anything else?"

"Yes," Roy said, "am at crash site of helicopter. Coordinates are... 58 degrees 41 seconds north, one hundred thirty seven degrees 45 seconds east at 7000 feet. Check it out as soon as possible."

"Roger, check crash at 58 degrees 41 seconds north, one- hundred thirty seven degrees 45 seconds east at 7000 feet. Any survivors?"

"No, over and out." Roy put the radio back in his parka. A few minutes later some rocks fell.

Kurt tugged on the rope three times. Roy untied and let go of his end. Kurt pulled the rope up. Seconds after the end of the rope disappeared Roy ducked as a small cascade of rocks showered down on him as Kurt rappelled down.

"Kurt!" Roy shouted. "Hold up a second. Let me get out of the way." The rocks stopped falling. Roy put on his pack and grabbed his ice axe, glissaded down fifty feet and traversed to the south, out of the path of falling rock.

"Okay, come on down."

Kurt had looped the rope around a skid on the helicopter and walked down the cliff letting the rope slide through the "Figure 8" on his harness. When he was fifteen feet above the lip of the serac he pushed off the face and let the rope slide rapidly. Roy could hear the sound of the rope sliding through Kurt's glove as Kurt arced away from the cliff and landed on the snow, avoiding the lip of the serac.

He picked up his ice axe and glissaded down holding on to one end of the rope. As he glissaded down the steep slope the loose end of the rope slithered up the cliff, around the frame of the helicopter that Kurt used for an anchor, and then dropped to the slope.

"What did you find?" Roy asked.

"Three dead. Two looked like they died in the crash. The third must have been sending the signal. The blood on the snow indicates he got out once and then got back into the bubble. Possibly to get out of the storm. Didn't do much good."

"How about the radio?"

"It was busted. Nothing seemed to work. One of the dead was impaled on the control panel so I couldn't get to the registration plate. Sorry."

"That's okay. We can contact the authorities when we get back and they can check it out. By the way, that was good climbing."

"Thanks. We had better start back."

"Kurt, I have a question concerning something in Ralph's diary. Ralph wrote he saw you in a rafting picture at a friend's house. How is that possible?"

Kurt smiled. "See if this explains." He unzipped his parka and removed a velcro wallet from an inner pocket. Kurt handed Roy a photograph.

Roy looked at two people sitting at a sidewalk table. They both looked like Kurt. "Twin brother?" Roy handed the picture back.

"Helmut, identical. He likes water, I like mountains."

The moon rose shortly after one in the morning and lit the glacier like a spotlight. Roy and Kurt trudged back along the trail they had blazed earlier.

The pace was brisk and methodical. Kurt was leading and there would be no worries about the route. Roy found his thoughts were scattered with visualization of the Wallace Images building, the assembly line, arguments among the staff and Tom's expressed sense of growing isolation. The route led them over a hidden crevasse and the snow crunched loudly in his subconscious. "Crunch," he thought. "Cohesive," he thought. A packed snow ball is a cohesive unit. The word cohesiveness resonated with each step until he found himself saying the word. "That's it," he said loud enough that Kurt shouted back

"What?"

"Nothing," Roy responded, "I am just starting to talk to myself."

"I know the feeling," Kurt responded. Neither of them had missed a step.

Roy recalled a four-day retreat two years before. A group of administrators from a nursing home and a retreat facilitator had decided to rough it, camping in the sand dunes at Assateague National Seashore in Maryland. Between swatting mosquitoes and green flies the facilitator discussed the rapid growth of the nursing home from one building, then two, then three over a period of six years. He had listened to some of the administrators complaining that they didn't get along with some of their old friends, people they had worked with for years. "We just don't see each other any more," was a common complaint.

The facilitator discussed a turn-of-the-century sociologist named Homans who believed that group cohesiveness was influenced by three factors – Friendliness, Interaction and Activity. The facilitator also indicated that a Nobel prizewinning Economist, Kenneth Arrow, had applied calculus to Homans parameters of cohesivenss to study how the three interacted with each other.

The theory had eluded the administrators but they did start to understand that people who were used to working in the same office might develop a sense of isolation if they were separated from their associates and moved to a new location. Since they did not bump into each other at coffee or passing in the hallways or rest rooms, the level of interaction decreased and with that the level of perceived friendliness. They met only at monthly program meetings when there were arguments about budget allocations and schedules.

The same thing was happening at Wallace Images. Tom's perception that Raymond Wallace had turned his back on Tom might be as simple as Tom being relocated to his own building. Raymond and Tom had worked side by side for years but for the past year they seldom saw each other. Tom's perception of Ralph's role as an internal spy probably reflected his growing paranoia about the loss of his only close friend. Who else was being isolated by the success at Wallace Images?

Roy almost talked to himself. He hummed his words to avoid disturbing Kurt or from being understood. The articulation forced a conscious level of attention. At the subconscious level there were too many fleeting ideas and images. "I will ask Brad about the expansion program and when different people started acting differently."

Once Roy focused on the idea of talking with Brad he relaxed and heard heard his feet pushing into the snow and his breathing. Roy and Kurt moved all night without stopping. They arrived at the Nunatak camp at 7:30 having marched over thirty-six miles.

Michael and Eugene already had the stoves going. The smell of coffee drifted through the camp area. It was quiet. Everyone else was in their tents.

CHAPTER 11
BRAD

———

"Bad news, boss." Juan greeted as he poked his head into the tent. Roy had just crawled in, spread his sleeping bag out and lay down to get half-an-hour of sleep. The sun warmed the inside of the tent and drew out the smell of dried sweat and sun cream. His arms and legs were growing heavy as they pressed into the nylon covered mound of down. One thought was on his mind. Sleep.

"Bad news. What do you mean?" He asked, eyes closed.

"Brad is dead," Juan said.

"What?" Roy sat up.

Juan crawled into the tent. "He fell into a serac. We haven't been able to get him out."

"How?"

"After you and Kurt left yesterday, we formed four teams to try to find the food supply. James, Ian and Eugene went around the north side on the glacier. Harry, Marcy and Mike went around the south side. I took Todd and Grant and went up on the south side of the rock. Tom and Brad went with us up to the base of the rock and then around the north side of the rock onto the plateau. They found the helicopter drop. Apparently they found the radio and were bringing it back here to camp and they fell."

"What do you mean, fell?"

"Well, they thought they could glissade or climb down the slope from the plateau straight into camp. It's steep where they tried to come down. It's a good slope to the left of where they were but the slope runs over a cliff a little to the right. It looked like they were too far to the right and slid over the cliff. Tom landed on a small rock shelf. Brad fell into the hole between the rock and the glacier. The rope jammed between two rocks and was cut by a sharp edge one of the rocks. Tom got banged up, cuts and bruises. I went down into the crack as far as I could. There was no sign of Brad."

Roy closed his eyes tightly. "Is this a bad dream? I'll wake up," he thought. He shook his head and crawled out of the tent. "Juan, take me to where they fell," he said as he put his boots on.

Roy and Juan stopped at Tom's tent. Kurt was there. Tom was telling him that Brad was dead and was startled as Roy pulled back the flap opening of the tent.

"I didn't know you were out there," he said.

"Just got here," Roy said, "I can see you are shaken up about Brad. Can you tell me how it happened?"

"It was steeper than we thought. We didn't know the cliff was so close. We thought there was snow all the way to the bottom." Tom looked at Roy, then at Kurt. "We were going to glissade but it got too steep. Brad was below me. He asked for a belay. I was getting ready to belay him when he slipped or fell. I couldn't really see him, it was so steep. The rope tangled on my foot and he pulled me down the slope as he fell.

It happened too fast. I slid past him and fell onto some rocks. I hit my head. Don't really know what happened. It felt like rocks and snow fell on me. He might have fallen on me too. I don't know if I was knocked out or not. Everything seems hazy. I called for him and found the rope. It looked cut where it was jammed between two rocks. Brad was gone. I think I passed out. The next thing I remember was Juan's face."

"Yeh," Juan said, "when the rest of us got back here and didn't find them we went looking. We could see tracks coming down the slope but they went into the rocks. Before I could start up Eugene had already found him and called down. When Grant and I got to Tom he was unconscious. At first I was afraid he was dead.

Eugene said he was still breathing. He had taken the rope off Tom's harness and put a sweater under his head. We didn't see Brad. When I got to Tom, I could see the rope in the rocks. Grant was really shaken up. He kept saying, "We have to find Brad.""

"Did you find the radio?" Roy asked Tom.

"Yes, but Brad had it in his pack when he fell." Tom stared at his knees, avoiding Roy's look. "It is terrible. What has happened is terrible."

Roy and Juan hiked up the slope toward the location where the accident had occurred. The route got progressively steeper. If they went straight up the slope they would miss the edge of the opening between the rock and snow. A few feet to the right of their path the serac opened.

"Strange," Roy said to Juan, "it looks like they would have missed the serac if they had come straight down. One of them moved to the right toward the rocks. The other's tracks come down over the rocks."

They climbed to the edge of the serac. There was a seven-foot gap between the snow and the rock. From camp the cliff was a rusty red color. Up close it looked like dirty black boulders that were held together by a reddish mud that had solidified and was now crumbling under the constant cycle of freezing and thawing.

"The dark rocks are almost pure iron and nickel," Roy commented. "The red basalt holding the dark rock erodes fast exposing the sharp edges." They climbed around the edge of the serac and onto the rock ledge where Juan had found Tom.

"This is where the rope was jammed and cut," Juan said kneeling and running his fingers over the dark rock. "It is sharp."

"Juan, when was the last time you cut a rope in two with a knife? How easy was it to do?"

"Pretty hard to cut. What are you saying?"

Roy ran his hand over the rocks where the rope had passed. "I think the rope was cut alright, but not necessarily by the rock."

"Are you saying Tom killed Brad? Is he the murderer? Why would he do it?

"I have an idea why Tom might be unhappy with the organization but it certainly doesn't provide motive for murder. In fact, I was going to talk with Brad about it today."

"The rope might already have been cut if somebody stepped on it with their crampons. It is possible the weak section caught in the rock. What did you do with the end that was tied to Tom."

"I don't know where it went." Juan gestured into the void. "I couldn't find it when I came up from down in there looking for Brad. It goes down a long ways. It was dark down there and too narrow for me to move around."

"Okay." Roy dropped a rock over the edge and listened for a sound. There was none. "Let's not suggest that it was anything more than an accident but keep your eye on Tom." They moved to the right onto the steep snow slope to head back to camp.

"What about the food supply?" Roy asked.

"We went up and got everything. There is enough for three to four days. It took several trips. We circled around and went up from the south side. Nobody wanted to come near this slope."

"Aren't we behind schedule?" Juan asked. "Will somebody start looking for us?"

"Not yet. We're only two days behind. Let's go. We have a long day ahead of us." Roy crouched, leaned back on his ice axe and let his feet slide down the slope like he was skiing. He corrected his speed by leaning back harder on the ice axe making turns and moving back and forth across the slope rather than going straight down the fall line. He could hear Juan glissading behind him. The sun had risen above the mountains to the east and the shadows covering the campsite were disappearing.

CHAPTER 12
ICEFALLS

Roy assigned the rope teams after they had breakfast, had taken down the tents and gotten their packs ready for travel.

Roy-Tom-Ian;
Eugene-Harry-Michael;
Juan-Todd-James;
Kurt-Marcy-Grant.

The sky was clear and the temperature in the camp area was just below freezing. As the sun rose the temperature would soar. The usual chatter between members of the group was missing. Conversation was limited to those few words needed to indicate they were ready to move. *Belay-on. Ready.*

The path northward from camp took them past several glacial ponds formed when the melting snow and ice ran down the glacier surface to a depression that did not have a crevasse running through it.

The water was crystal clear and the bottom and walls were blue. It was a little after 8:30 when they moved down a gentle slope at the base of the Nunatak, onto a field of crevasses which were bigger than any they had seen. Most of the crevasses were in a north-to-south direction crossing the flow of ice. Others ran west to east. A portion of the glacier looked like long stair steps with four to five terraces of ice running parallel to each other. Each terrace step was thirty to fifty feet high with a bottomless crevasse in front. There were subway-size tunnels going into the walls.

After forty-five minutes they stopped. They were getting warm from the continuous exertion, the rising sun and the rays reflecting off the snow. Everyone mechanically took off their heavy parka, took a sip of water, rubbed sun cream on their faces, behind their ears, under their chins and up their nostrils, then put their packs on and waited.

"Boss," Juan, standing near Roy said, "it sure seems quiet. No complaining about heavy packs or blisters."

The realization that three people were dead seemed to separate each person.

"I have slides of a helicopter flying into tunnels like those," Roy said loudly. "Since there are no trees or objects that we can use as a reference it is hard to tell how big things are or how far away they are." Nobody asked any questions and the group moved on.

It took three hours to work their way past the large crevasses and turn westward. They had skirted around the eastern side of Mt. LaPerouse and would follow a long sloping glacier that eventually became a three-thousand-foot icefall. Up until this point in the trip most travel had been on relatively flat glacier surface with mounds and high spots where the ice flowed over sub-surface rock formations. Now every step was uphill. The general slope was uniform but the surface was carved by the sun's rays into a scalloped pattern called sun cups. Dust blowing off the ridges settles on the surface and absorbs more sunlight than the ice and melts into the surface.

Rocks that had rolled off a higher ridge and landed on hard ice eventually melt into the glacier. The sun's rays coming from the east warm the east side of the rocks, which in turn melts the ice on the east side and the rock then rolls into the hole where the ice had been. The mountains to the west block the sun in the evening so the rocks could not melt their way back to their starting point.

Rain coming from one direction can also cause the rocks to move in that direction. The rain hits one side and runs off the rock. The water running off the rock melts the ice and the rock rolls into the hole.

On the lower reaches of the approach to the icefalls the sun cups were the size of regular stairs and walking was relatively easy.

"Remember the rest step!" Roy yelled back across the distance of four rope teams. "Lift, Step, relax, breathe. Lift, step, relax, breathe. We are gaining altitude and you have to suck in more air to get the same amount of oxygen. Every day that you gain altitude your body starts to generate more red blood cells to grab the oxygen that is in the rarified air."

The sun cups changed from stair steps, to chair high, to the height of small tables. Once the steps became high enough, water would collect in them and eventually break over the rim and erode a crack in the sun cup. The pattern of sun cups evolved into a pattern of ankle-wide trenches that ran down the glacier. It was difficult to step into and out of these trenches. The rate of travel was reduced to a crawl over one trench into another. They would follow one trench uphill for a ways until it pinched out, then climb into another one.

It took an hour and a half to reach the base of the icefalls where they stopped for a rest.

"That was exhausting," James said as he dropped his pack. The others grunted acknowledgment. Kurt arrived and coiled up the rope as Marcy and Grant joined the group.

"We started at eight-thirty," Michael observed, looking at his watch. "Except for one quick break we have traveled for four and a half hours without stopping."

"Kurt, Juan," Roy said, "it is going to take eight to nine hours to work our way through the mess above us. There is no one path. We can tackle it in three directions. If we get to a place were there is nothing but a blank wall then Kurt or I will have to climb it, and everybody will use their ascenders to get up."

"Listen up," Roy changed his focus to the whole group, "don't think of this as an insurmountable challenge. Think of it as a giant amusement park where you get to climb all you want. Rest awhile. We'll start in half an hour. With luck we get to the top before it gets too dark to climb but there is a good chance we will have to bivouac."

The icefalls looked like a jumbled pile of ice cubes twenty to fifty feet high. There was no regular pattern as to how they were oriented. It was sometimes possible to walk up the top of one that was sloping in one direction and climb up three feet to the next one that sloped in another direction. At times it was possible to cut footsteps into the side of a block to get to the top. At other times, Roy or Kurt used an ice-climbing hammer that looked like short ice axe. The head had a blade on one side and a hammer head on the other. They would reach up, drive the hammer blade into the wall, lift a leg and kick the toe points of their crampons into the face and lift up, then repeat the process with the other hand and leg.

They normally used this technique if they had to climb only ten or twelve feet. Rather than climb vertically they preferred to explore another set of blocks to climb. There were no rules that a direct route had to be taken. Sometimes they would climb down to a block that would lead to another series of blocks that would move then higher up the ice falls. There always was the chance that the path taken would end up in a dead end.

Roy could sometimes see that the path that Kurt or Juan was taking would lead to an impassible block of ice or crevasse and would yell across to let them know. At times Kurt or Juan would warn Roy of problems on a route.

After climbing a thousand vertical feet the teams all came to the same ramp of ice and faced a sixty-foot, near vertical ice wall that was slightly overhanging the last twenty feet. The overhanging section was not solid ice but compressed snow from the past two years. Kurt looked at Roy and said, "Your turn."

"While I am trying to get up this thing, you should eat. It is already 4:30. It will be a very long day and we won't have a chance to set up camp."

Roy tied a narrow line to his harness. "When I get up to the snow section I will want to pull up two ice axes. Until then I will use the ice hammers and ice screws."

He approached the base of the cliff and started up the same as he had been doing on the small vertical sections below. Now, however, he put in ice screws every eight feet. While he hammered in the molybdenum screws that were slotted, half-inch tubes with deep threads on the outside, he would hang on to one ice hammer by one hand and use the other to attach the line going to the other hammer to his harness so he could sit in it. This freed one hand to place the screw in. Once he had driven the screw in he attached a carabineer and then clipped the climbing rope to it. This was time consuming and tiring.

Every time he chopped at the wall with the ice hammer, a shower of ice would rain down on those sitting below.

An ice screw was placed just below the top of the last layer of solid ice. Roy hung by the carabineer, asked that ice axes be tied to the light line, then pulled them up. Reaching up as high as he could he scooped out a small pocket from the snow where he drove the shaft of the ice axe into the snow. Just below that and slightly to the right side he scooped out a second pocket where he could place his right foot. He drove the ice axe into the top pocket up to the head and looped the climbing rope around the shaft twice. Walking on his crampon toe points and partially chinning himself, he put his right foot into the lower pocket and stood so that his waist was just below the ice axe. If he stood any higher the ice axe would have been pulled out.

He held the loops around the shaft with his right hand so the rope wouldn't slide while he carved two more pockets for his left foot and the other ice axe. When he was able to loop the rope around the second ice axe, he pulled out the first one, and repeated the process of scooping out pockets and hammering in the ice axe. The process was methodical, almost mechanical.

"He seems to know what he is doing," Grant said.

"Yes, and he seems to be enjoying himself," Michael added ducking some of the snow that was spraying out from the overhang. "If I am not mistaken he is singing."

Juan said, "Roy likes to hum Ravel's 'Bolero' as he climbed because of its constant beat. Whenever he starts up a slope he always remembers his girl friend from when he was climbing as a teenager. One day he was leading a climb up a slope and started going faster and faster. She asked why he was speeding up. He responded by saying he was climbing to a tune called 'The Bolero,' the ultimate seduction music. She laughed and told him to listen to it again. The essence of 'The Bolero' she said was its constant beat. The music only got louder, not faster. Since then he has used it as his metronome while climbing."

The tensions of the morning had passed. They looked at the sheer wall in front of them and knew that from then on they had to work together.

Once on top of the block Roy drove in a large anchor and belayed Kurt up. Kurt removed the ice screws as he ascended. When he came over the edge he looked at Roy and said, "Impressive."

"Thank you."

Kurt moved south about ten feet, set up an anchor and dropped a rope down. He pulled his pack up, dropped the rope again and hoisted another pack. Marcy attached her ascender to the rope and climbed. She had pulled a rope up with her and used it to haul up packs when she was on top. Tom had attached his ascender to Roy's rope and climbed up. He helped Marcy pull up packs until others arrived. Forty minutes later everybody was on top with all the packs.

"That took an hour-and-a-half," Roy commented. "I hope we don't have any many more like it."

Kurt observed, "That looked like the worst of it. The next fifteen hundred feet tapers off a little. We do have a cruddy looking pile of rock at the top."

"That will be your department," Roy said smiling.

"Let's go." Roy tied himself back into the rope for climbing and started up the sloping block in front of him.

Progress was slow but steady. The gloom of the morning had passed. The repetitive process of climbing and belaying one another brought them back to a cooperating group.

Marcy said to Kurt, "These blocks of ice look like slices of cake with chocolate frosting."

He nodded, and replied, "You are getting hungry," and kept climbing.

Juan was climbing onto the same block that Marcy was on. "Each layer of frosting marks the beginning of summer. During summer the dust blows on. During the winter the snow piles up. Then it all gets compressed by the snow the next year."

"I get it, like rings in a tree."

The sun had passed overhead and was already low in the western sky, blocked from view by the ridge they were climbing. They could see the long shadow from the peaks above them spread across the glacier toward the gray peaks in the east.

They had been climbing in the shadow of the ridge above them for an hour when Grant stumbled and grabbed his left leg. Juan yelled to Roy above him that there was a problem and climbed down to Grant.

"What's wrong?"

"Leg cramp. I am not used to doing anything like this."

Roy yelled down to find out what the problem was and Juan described it.

"Drink some water and lick some salt. Juan, massage his leg. Distribute some of his gear to a couple of the others. Kurt is going to need a strong team going up the face so let's move Ian off my rope and put him on Kurt's rope."

Juan asked, "Did you say replace Grant with Ian?"

"Yes," Roy answered, "replace Grant with Ian."

"I'll be okay, I can make it," Grant said weakly to Juan. Juan took the rope off Grant's harness and clipped him onto the end of Roy's rope.

"Ha!" Harry chided, "he's already afraid Ian will take his place in the office."

"Shut up, Harry," James snapped.

Juan called over to Michael who was sitting near Grant. "Michael, take the tent Grant is carrying in order to lighten his pack."

"Why should I?" Michael said defiantly.

Todd, who had been subdued since Ralph's death erupted, "You arrogant prick!" He stood and stepped toward Michael, who started to arise.

Roy jerked on Todd's harness keeping Todd off balance as he grabbed for Michael's throat. Todd fell on Michael and with his teeth clenched whispered from deep inside himself; "Because your pack is lighter and Grant can use your help."

Michael stared at him wide-eyed and backed away as far has he could from his sitting position. Without saying anything further he reached his left arm out and took the tent that Juan handed him.

Roy said quietly to himself, "That is communicating," then louder to the rest of the group, "Kurt is at the base of the rock cliff. It is going to be awhile before Grant has to climb. Move over and get behind that block to the north so you are protected from rock fall. The ridge is rotten. Also, Marcy, trade places with Tom."

Kurt, Tom and Ian moved up the slope to the beginning of the steep cliff. Kurt studied the rock above him. There was a series of ledges that sloped downward to the right. That would be good because as the group climbed one person did not have to climb directly above another. There were some short vertical sections where Kurt could put in pitons for protection.

Roy suggested that Kurt also put some extra pitons in for a hand line. The group was not experienced in mountaineering and they were now looking down several thousand feet.

Most of the time in the icefalls there wasn't a sensation of being up high. It was just a series of small ledges, small challenges and the vertical exposure was minimal. As they started up the near-vertical rock barrier the exposure was overwhelming.

Kurt reached a smooth blank section that had a seven-inch ledge and no handholds. They had to take off their packs and haul them across when they reached the other side.

Harry was the first to express doubts that he could climb the rock. Grant and James followed in their concern. Eugene crossed and pulled over Harry and Michael's packs. Harry stood to approach the small ledge and moved his left foot onto it. He looked down and moaned, "I can't do it."

"What a wimp," Marcy mocked. "You stay here Harry, I'll fill in for you back at the Office."

"You'd like that wouldn't you?" Harry sucked in a couple of breaths. "But I won't give you the satisfaction." He started a slow two-step shuffle across the seven-inch rock ledge with his nose pressed against the rock. When the steepness tapered off a little and the ledge widened an inch he looked down. They had moved to the left far enough so that the ice falls were no longer under them. He noticed that a rock he kicked fell eight hundred feet before bouncing and going another thousand feet. He tried to watch it after it bounced but felt his stomach churn. He pressed his forehead against the rock.

Roy yelled across to him, "Harry, breathe deep a couple of times. Don't hold your breath. You have to look at you feet so you don't slip on a rock."

"I'm stuck," he cried.

Eugene called over to him, "Relax, Harry, I have you on belay. You can't fall."

"Can I have your leather posture chair redone in velvet?" Marcy called over to him.

"You bitch," he muttered and continued the traverse to the other side.

Michael followed Harry. Juan had retied his rope so Michael could belay him. Juan crossed and Todd followed quickly, seemingly without concern.

James looked at Todd and said, "If you and Harry can do it so can I."

James was halfway across the ledge when a dull grinding sound came out of the rock. The ledge lurched slightly. A small earthquake jolted the ridge causing rocks to cascade down the slope. Rocks bounced over the ledge and flew into the space below with a fluttering sound. James screamed, "I'm falling." He fell twelve feet and swung into the rocky wall below Todd.

Todd looked down and said, "I've got you. I didn't kill Ralph and I'm not going to let you fall."

Roy yelled across the face to see if anyone was hurt in the rock fall. Everybody called back saying they were okay.

James found some foot holds and climbed up while Todd pulled up the slack rope. Juan patted Todd on the back and said, "Good work. You saved his life."

When James crawled onto the wider ledge he embraced Todd and with tears flowing down his cheeks said, "Thank you, thank you."

The climb to the top of the ridge and across a large snowfield went without further incident.

"Everybody, I think we should all give thanks to our guide," Roy said when Grant, the last person on his rope, reached the top. "Thank you, Kurt."

Everyone took turns shaking Kurt's hand and said, "Thanks."

They were at eight thousand feet looking down six thousand feet on the east side and across a flat snowfield to the Pacific Ocean twelve miles to the west.

Roy hiked a hundred yards across the snow-field to where it started to drop to the west and took off his pack. "Home for the night. Be it ever so humble and high. We are guarded on the south by Mt. LaPerouse and to the north by Mt. Dagelet."

"Wow," was the general expression as the last edge of the sun dropped behind the horizon of the Pacific Ocean. A menagerie of animal-shaped clouds turned bright pink, then dark red, then gray. The sun set.

Marcy walked over to Kurt. "Are we tent mates tonight?" She asked.

He looked at her and then at Tom. "Not tonight. I have to finish a chess game with Tom that we started a couple of nights ago."

She looked at him, puzzled. "I have been stood up," she announced. "Who can I sleep with tonight?"

There was chorus of "Not me." started by Ian.

Marcy went over to help James massage his cramped leg. He was able to recover enough to get to the top but was in pain. "Not me."

"Knock it off," she said, "I'm just trying to be helpful."

Michael, James and Eugene started the stoves and the others set up the tents. Roy warned them to anchor the tents with ice screws because they were up where the winds could blow fairly hard.

Roy went to Marcy. "You did a good job of motivating Harry down there. You sure know how to push a guy's buttons. Thanks. You can use my tent."

She looked at him for a few seconds. "Thank you."

James looked at the two of them. "Did I miss something."

Juan came over. "Boss, do you hear a helicopter out there?" He pointed east in the direction of the crashed helicopter.

"Yep."

"Roy," Michael addressed as he stood a few feet back from Juan and Roy until Juan had finished speaking.

"Yes, Michael?"

"Can I talk to you?" He motioned he wanted to move away from the group.

"I guess I have been a real jerk."

"What do you mean?" Roy asked.

"I've been hearing what others say. I have for years, but, it has been different here. Being called bull-headed or whatever doesn't mean anything to me. I can usually close the door and figure out how to make things work in the office. Here it just stops. You saved my life a couple of days ago. I never thanked you for it. Today, down there, Todd caught my attention. I've never had anything like that happen before. Out here you are in charge, you know what you are doing. That has always been my role. Not any more."

"How do you mean?"

"My father died when I was seven. I had two brothers, three and five, and a sister, one. My mother said I was in charge of them since I was the oldest. If there was a problem she told me to go to my room and figure it out then come and do what had to be done. As Jake, John and Roberta, my brothers and sister grew older they called me a jerk, Mr. Know-it-all and a variety of epithets. Whatever they said, I still found ways to solve the problems that arose because of their actions and other circumstances."

"What about your mother?"

"She worked hard and seemed to be sick a lot. Later I found she had an alcohol problem. Sometimes I really had to work hard to keep the others from setting her off. If there was a problem she said I was in charge and they were my problem."

"What did your dad do?"

"He was an electrical engineer. He was great. I was operating a ham radio from the time I could remember. I am told I knew Morse code before I knew the alphabet. All that seemed to pass after he died. I always wanted to be the engineer that he was.

"In high school I didn't have time for sports with doing my homework and helping my brothers and sister. Somewhere they developed the idea that someone was supposed to do everything for them.

I guess I didn't know how to raise them. I never married. I didn't want to raise another family."

Roy watched Michael. Michael paused and looked back across the Brady glacier and the icefall they had climbed.

"Sounds like you aren't too open to teamwork," Roy said casually.

"I guess it depends on how you define teamwork. Never like this. Teamwork usually has meant setting out the tasks for others to do. Maybe others have had good ideas that I should have listened to but somehow I equated them with my brothers and sister. If I didn't go along with them they just called me names. Sometimes the work is just like being home again. When people start yelling I close my office door."

"Well, Michael, out here there is only one room and we are all in it. You're an engineer and you know about trade-offs."

"Sure."

"When others are involved their ideas represent trade-off options that should be considered," Roy continued. "Just because you didn't think of it doesn't mean it isn't valid or that their idea means yours isn't any good. There is a difference, however, between here, getting up that icefall for instance, and an engineering project back at the office. Here we have the same objective. In the office everybody has a different objective that they are charged with. They have different organizational objectives, not necessarily personal objectives."

"I'm not sure what you are driving at," Michael said.

"Harry as budget manager has the objective of minimizing cost as his organizational responsibility. Research has an objective to push the technology no matter what the cost. That is their job. The project manager, you, is stuck trying to find the balance, the trade- off, between the competing objectives. For every level of technological capability there is a cost. The more advanced the technology the higher the cost. The key is finding the balance between cost and performance that represents what must be achieved to win the competition."

"The reasons for the trade-off need to be spelled out so the opposing sides know why the decision was made, otherwise the whole project decision process looks like a series of unilateral decisions. If the reasons are made clear then grousing by others about what might have been represents personal cheap shots on their part."

"Tom always wants to push new ideas."

"Good. Somebody, you or James, if he is now in charge, has to convince him that him new ideas are needed. They do not have to be new products. Proposals but represent profitable revisions to existing products and contracts."

"Keep in mind that the process of making trade-offs can involve intense and heated debates. The processes is best kept open with everybody involved. There are no stone tablets coming down from on high in project management. If there is a lot of debate it probably means there are uncertainties. The battles should be about how to reduce the uncertainty and not about who is right. There is no right or wrong, only outcomes."

"What you suggest is interesting. Where did you get your ideas?" Michael asked.

"We have had a lot of project manager problems argued out while hanging off of ropes."

"What?"

"These ideas emerge on trips like this one. Sooner or later people start saying what they are really feeling."

Michael looked down the icefalls then changed his gaze to the west to the sunset over the ocean. "I'll try to make my processes more collaborative. The guys aren't my little brothers and sister. If I accept what they said about the crystals, I really screwed up.

The company really is nearly bankrupt because of it."

CHAPTER 13
MT. DAGELET

"This is the first night in ten days we have watched a sunset, brief as it was, when the sun did set. There has always been a mountain in the way. It's like being home," Ian observed, raising his coffee cup to west.

"When did you ever watch the sun set at home?" Marcy sat down next to him on a rock that was lying on the ice. "You were always working on something to make Grant look foolish."

"That isn't the case. I am not trying to upstage Grant. He runs the mainframe and I am interested in distribution of computation capability. He is a neatnick, I'm more casual."

"What are we doing? Watching the sunset or taking shots at Grant?" James asked as he joined Ian and Marcy. He limped as he found a rock to sit on and carried it back to Ian and Marcy. He dropped it near Marcy where he could sit and face Ian.

"Watching the sunset," Marcy said.

"It's only eleven o'clock and I'm tired already. All we did was hike for three hours and climb six thousand feet in ten intense hours. I must be getting old," James said. "I've never worked so hard in my life. I didn't think I was going to have the strength to get up that last cliff. That was awesome."

"You are limping," Marcy noted. "What happened?"

"I fell off a ledge. Bumped my leg. No big deal," James said. "It should be okay by morning. Where are Michael, Grant and the others?"

Marcy looked at him for a few seconds and shook her head. "Jim," she started to say,

"James," he corrected, looking at her. "My name is James."

"Look, Jim," she shot back, "a whole bunch of things have been changing and a whole bunch of things should be obvious by now. For starters, since your brother is dead you are going to be in charge. Second, there are some people in the group who don't get along with each other and never have."

Juan came out of his tent and found a place to sit next to Ian. "What's going on?" he asked Ian quietly.

"Don't know yet. I was watching the sun set."

"I'd prefer to be called James," James said. "I was not going to assume leadership until we got back to the office and paid the proper respects to Raymond.

Then I'll take over." He dropped his voice and paused for several seconds. "I don't know what you mean about people not getting along."

"I'm here, Harry isn't. Ian is here, Grant isn't. Grant is paranoid about Ian." Marcy sucked in some of the thin air and shot her words at James. "Harry is paranoid about me. Tom is paranoid about Michael. Half the key staff, your staff, is afraid of the other half."

"I think you are exaggerating." James stood as he focused on her. "They have some professional differences of opinion. We will deal with that back in the office. I'm going to bed." He limped to his tent.

"Leaders are born," Marcy said shaking her head. "There is a sample of stillbirth."

"Why should Harry be intimidated by you?" Ian asked.

"Because he is a junkie and he knows that I know. Now you know." She paused. "Harry!" she shouted, "I told them you are a junkie. You can relax now."

Roy was descending from the ridge above camp and walked over to the group. Grant crawled out of his tent. Eugene was already out of his tent talking to Harry. They walked over to Marcy. Tom and Kurt did not come out of their tent.

Harry was shaking and breathing hard. He clenched his fist and stepped toward Marcy.

James had come back from his tent. He grabbed Harry's arm and said to Marcy, "Explain yourself."

Marcy looked quickly at each person in the group, all either sitting or standing in a semicircle around her. She caught Harry's eye and said she had been working in a drug abuse rehabilitation center in Boulder, Colorado as the accountant two years before. Harry's eyes widened and he stepped back from the group.

"Harry was one of the patients. A skier from a group staying at a lodge in Aspen several months before had raped my sister. I had tracked down the group and it was someone from Wallace Images. When I saw Harry's name on the roster at the rehab center I knew I had a way of getting a job with Wallace Images and could track down the person who raped my sister. I blackmailed Harry into getting me a job at Wallace. Now, Harry, you don't have to worry any more. I don't have any more secrets."

To the north an avalanche thumped and clattered off the slopes of Mt. Dagelet. The wind slapped the open flaps of the tents and rippled over the rip-stop nylon, buffeting the fabric. Nobody said anything. Harry stared at the snow at his feet.

Todd walked over from his tent. "Marcy, how can you be so cruel?" he said as he went to Harry, stood in front of him and grabbed his parka above the elbow. "Harry, Harry," he shook Harry's arm, "you tell us what is going on."

Harry looked up, grimaced, forced a smile and told the group that he had picked up a drug habit during the period when Wallace was having problems with the communicator. Brad had arranged for a treatment program and told everyone that he, Harry, was taking care of his sick mother in Colorado.

He confessed that he had bypassed regular security procedures to get Marcy hired. "She never told me about her sister or why she wanted to join Wallace. She just insisted."

Juan interjected, "You cured now?"

"Yes, I haven't had a drug problem since getting back. It has been rough at times but I haven't touched anything."

James stepped toward Marcy and looked at Harry. "Harry, I don't think any of us feels differently about you and maybe this will help us understand some of the things that have happened at the office. I guess we are better off having this out in the open. Maybe we should even thank Marcy."

"Marcy," he asked, "have you found out who raped your sister?"

"No," she answered, "not yet. I'm not sure I will. Maybe he isn't with Wallace."

Nobody said anything as they went back to their tents.

Juan walked over to Roy. "Some fireworks! What time do we get up?"

"Today was a rough day. Let's let everyone sleep in, get rested. Tomorrow won't be quite as tough but we do have a lot of ground to cover. We will swing around the north side of Dagelet and get on top of the ridge that separates the La Perouse glacier system from the Crillon glacier system. That is going to be rotten rock, and tricky."

Roy crawled into his tent, and sat at the edge of the opening while he took his boots off. Marcy had already put her sleeping bag in the tent and was sitting in it.

"Don't turn around," she said, "I not decent yet. Kurt told me that I should take off my tight things before I get into my sleeping bag. That way I won't have my circulation restricted during the night and get cold."

"I've heard that," Roy said, "it's one of the better lines."

"You mean it is not true?" she said sliding into her sleeping bag?

Roy turned around and sat on his bag. "Your turn, don't look." He took his pants off and put his legs into his bag. He took his shirt off and rolled it up with his pants to make a pillow. "There is some merit to the idea."

"You know you were pretty rough on Harry out there," Roy said as he lay on his side facing her with his head propped up, leaning on an elbow.

She rose up facing him. Her sleeping bag was not closed. In the dim light left after the sunset and before the last rays disappeared from the western horizon he could see the outline of her breasts. She moved closer. He could feel the warmth stored in her down sleeping bag radiate from the opening.

"I was getting tired of holding back, of keeping a secret. Sometimes holding onto things gets in the way of moving ahead. Keeps us from doing what we want."

She put her head on the edge of his sleeping bag. When he put his head down, the top of her head pressed against his cheek. In the confinement of the sleeping bag he had nowhere to put the arm he was leaning on except around her sleeping bag.

"Go to sleep he said. It will be a long day tomorrow."

"Yes," she said softly. She moved closer to him under the slight touch of his arm around her. The slight draft of cold air that seeped into her bag as she opened it to pull his bag over her warmed quickly.

"Sleep," He said, as she lowered her cheek to his chest and put a warm hand on his stomach and exhaled.

"Oh, you found the king," he heard Tom say to Kurt as the wind blew the sound of his voice toward Roy's tent.

Roy strained to hear more and rose slightly to put his ear above the edge of the sleeping bag. Marcy's hand rubbed across his stomach several times and moved lower brushing against the thickening hair.

"Lie down and go to sleep," she said blowing softly.

CHAPTER 14
SOUTH CRILLON GLACIER

Roy opened his eyes. The tent was dark. A gentle breeze from the west buffeted the fabric. Marcy's hair lay across his chest, her head on his right arm. He raised his left arm and checked the time on the glowing dial of his watch. Two A.M.. He eased his arm from under her head and whispered, "Party break." Slowly he got out of his sleeping bag and slipped on his shirt and pants.

He unzipped the tent flap and crawled out to put on his socks and boots. Dressed, he stepped quietly toward the latrine area but continued past it, climbing a small slope to where he could overlook the Brady Glacier to the east. It seemed to glow dimly in the starlight.

"Hello, Looker. This is Ghostwalker." He spoke softly into the small microphone and pointed the fountain-pen-sized transmitter toward the middle star in Orion's belt. He thought he shouldn't have gotten distracted during the night. At best the satellite would be visible for transmission for a twenty-minute period. Now he had only a few minutes left.

"Ghostwalker;" The response came back. Ghostwalker was the signal that they were to use above the Brady Glacier on the western slopes. "Good to hear from you. Not much time. You have a problem. We think.." Static interrupted the transmission and then faded. "..killed.." Another burst of static. Former..." The signal got weaker with the static. "... covert operations. Now industrial espionage."

"Say again. I didn't get the name." Roy transmitted but realized the signal was gone.

He climbed back to the latrine area and headed for the tents trying to avoid waking the others. As he passed the tent used by Michael and Eugene, Michael said, "That took long enough. Do you feel okay?" as he opened the tent flap. "Roy! I thought you were Eugene. Is he okay? He has been gone for a long time."

Roy crouched in front of Michael, turned on his flashlight, and looked into the tent. "When did he leave?"

"It seems like a half-an-hour or more. He said he was going to pee. I was starting to wonder if he was having a problem."

Roy yelled, "Everybody up." He moved to the next tent, unzipped the flap, and shoved his flashlight inside. Harry and James blinked in the light. James asked, "What is the matter?"

Todd and Grant emerged from the second tent that Roy approached. Roy didn't say anything and continued to the next tent. Juan and Ian crawled out of the tent to Roy's left.

"What up, boss?" Juan asked. Roy opened the tent belonging to Kurt and Tom. It was empty. By now everyone else was out of his or her tent. Tom, Kurt and Eugene were gone.

"I think Eugene is an industrial spy and is responsible for the accidents. It looks like he has taken Kurt to get off the peak and Tom as hostage. Pack up. We have to try and catch up with them."

"How do we know which way they went?" Juan asked.

"From the map there appears to be only one feasible route." Roy set the map down so he and Juan could study it. Juan held the flashlight while Roy pointed to the route. "We take the glacier north, climb this ridge above the ice falls. On the other side of the ridge is a small glacier that descends to the South Crillon glacier. There appear to be three steep snowfields from the base of the ridge to the glacier. We will know in a few hours when we get to the top of the ridge. Pack up," Roy repeated.

"What about Kurt's tent?"

"Leave it."

Marcy commented after they had been hiking for a few minutes. "We haven't traveled at night before. It is kind of eerie. Why can't we use our flashlights?"

"Your eyes have gotten used to the starlight. In a little while the moon will be out. A flashlight would blind your night vision.

Beside, if Eugene is looking back he might see a light."

The surface was firm and smooth. It angled slightly to the northwest. A few rocks from the surrounding ridges had rolled onto the surface. Occasionally somebody would hit a rock with his or her ice axe. It sounded like a clapper hitting the side of the bell. The sound reverberated in the still morning air. They would mutter, "Sorry."

The sun had risen east of the Brady. By the time they reached the base of the ridge they had to start climbing. The morning sky was bright but the ridge blocked the sun's rays.

The ridge had the consistency of a large pile of loose rubble. Large and small rocks were piled on top of one another. Every step forced a rock loose. It would roll down the slope and knock others loose to start a small dusty avalanche.

The nine traveled diagonally up to the right trying to be careful to not kick rocks down on top of the others. By moving diagonally they avoided hitting each other. When it was necessary to change direction they would all come together before Roy started up in the new direction. A rusty-colored volcanic dust cloud rose from the small rock avalanches and caught the first rays of the sun when they were halfway up the ridge.

They were not roped in even though the slope was steep and descended several thousand feet. A rope would have snagged rocks and made travel more difficult. Roy showed them that they could travel just as they did on steep snow using the ice axe as an outrigger on the uphill side, poking the pick end into the slope between the loose rocks. "If your foot slips, lean on the ice axe. It will become your third leg."

The nine worked their way back and forth up the slope for two hours before resting. Once they stopped, they could hear some of the larger rocks they had knocked loose still rattling down the slope.

"Hey Boss," Juan said, "you would make a good Indian tracker. That looks like the tracks of the others. But it only looks like the tracks of two people. Where's number three, up front scouting the route?"

"Remember, my south-of-the-border friend, I am part Indian." Roy pointed to the east. "It looks like there are some recently rolled rocks over there. Might be natural or it might be number three.

These two are taking a more direct route up the slope. It was faster. They didn't have to worry about knocking the rocks onto each other."

They group resumed their ascent. Everybody was learning to place their feet on the uphill side of smaller rocks with a quick push-down. The smaller rocks seemed to lock together. The larger rocks rolled under their ankles and pushed other rocks down the slope.

The top of the ridge varied in width. In places it was only one boulder wide with the boulder poised to roll down one side or the other depending on which way the wind blew hardest. Other places were fifteen to twenty feet wide. Looking down to the north they saw a glacial cirque, a horseshoe-shaped valley that opened to the northwest. A larger glacier or ice cap that covered the area originally had carved it out. When the ice melted the valley was exposed leaving a series of steep snowfield terraces. Eight hundred feet below them the upper snow field ran upward to their right and butted up against a cliff.

The cliff was topped by an icefall flowing from the end of the glacier they had traveled on during the dim hours of the morning. A small waterfall trickled down the cliff and disappeared under the snow slope. It fed a small intermittent river that ran down the rock under the snow slope and eventually into the labyrinthine water passages under the glaciers below. The northern edge of the snow terrace was edged by a crevasse. that was formed as a field of ice pulled away from the slope under the continuous pull of gravity.

At the moment a large precariously balanced block of snow and ice was connected to the upper slope with a sinuous bridge of snow. In a few more days the block would break off the edge and cascade three hundred feet to the next snow terrace. The lower terrace flowed gently for half-a-mile before beginning a steep descent to still another cliff.

Just above the edge of the snow slope they were climbing down toward was an opening to a tunnel that ran into the slope. It was formed by the flow of water down the cliff cutting under the avalanche debris from the glacier above. Across the snow slope from the ridge they were descending was a steep slope with a vertical "V" gully under a small icefall from another glacier.

A large block of ice had wedged in the gully and dammed the progress of small avalanches of snow and rock. When the block melted, the block material would tumble down and across the front of the terrace. Water running under the edges of the block suggested that an avalanche could happen at any time. The chances would increase as soon as the sun's rays hit the slope.

They had to descend the slope they were on and cross the terrace under the plugged slope, then climb down a steep ramp of rock to the terrace below. On the block of ice connected to the broken edge of the terrace they had to cross lay a body. It was face down, clothed in a red parka.

Harry said, "That must be Tom. He is the only one with a red parka. Kurt's was a rust color and Eugene's was green. Is he alive?"

The descent to the terrace was similar to the climb but downward and more difficult. The rocks were just as unstable and each person created a small avalanche with every step.

Roy studied the slope as they descended drawing an imaginary dotted path in his mind which zigagged down the slope. He needed a route that kept rock fall to the left of the terrace and would provide access to the narrow edge of the terrace in front of the tunnel opening.

No one spoke as they descended. The red form remained motionless.

As they proceeded to the right they could see more glacial terraces descending to the main glacier four thousand feet below. Rocks flowing down the southern slope of Mt. Crillon had painted the northern edge of the glacier brown. Four brown ribbons of rock running the length of the glacier were evenly spaced across its half-mile width. At least four other glaciers had flowed together to form the one below them.

Minerals found on the piles of rock forming the ribbons could be traced "upstream" from one glacial valley to another to the slope that originally spawned them. Rocks holding the minerals were deposited on the lateral moraine on the edge of glacier. When two glaciers flow together the lateral moraines merged into a ribbon of rock that was in the middle of the large glacier.

A hundred feet from the terrace a red stain in the snow was visible. As they came together to make their last change in direction Ian asked quietly, almost to himself. "Is that blood?" Nobody answered.

They reached the edge of the terrace ramp. Tom lay twelve feet away from them on the block of snow connected to the terrace in front tunnel by a thin narrow eight-foot snow bridge.

Roy wondered if the narrow bridge of snow connecting the block to the ramp was strong enough to hold him. How did the body get onto the block? He probed with his ice axe and worked himself toward the edge of the ramp. The edge of the ramp was overhung three feet to where it connected to the snow bridge. He saw that another bridge had been cut away. The body had been placed on the block as a trap.

"Juan, go up to tunnel opening and belay me. This edge is overhanging and not too stable. It looks like they cut out the bridge used to put Tom out there. I'll try to crawl out to Tom."

"Everybody, go with Juan. Get behind him in the tunnel. You will have less exposure to rock fall." Roy uncoiled a rope, handed one end to Juan and tied the other end to his harness. Roy hoped that the bridge would hold if he lay down and distributed his weight over a wide enough area. If he could get his ice axe onto the other side he could ease his way onto the block. He waited for Juan to set up the belay.

Juan climbed up to the tunnel and positioned himself inside the opening so he could belay Roy. He sat and brace his feet against edge of the opening. The others climbed past him.

Grant noticed aloud, "There are two waterfalls on the cliffs above that flow under this slope. This tunnel must go down to the river."

"Wow!" Mary said as she entered the opening. "It looks like a New York subway tunnel in here."

Todd asked, "Where is the graffiti?"

"This must be twenty feet wide and the ceiling is close to fifteen feet high," Ian said. "I wonder how far back it goes."

"I can hear water running back there," Harry said as he climbed over some ice blocks and disappeared from the bright light.

Grant advised that they should stay together. He moved into the opening ten feet and sat down and turned his back to the cold air flowing out from inside.

"Belay on!" Juan yelled to Roy.

Roy knelt down in front of the bridge and began to slide onto it like a diver in slow motion. If he had put crampons on he could pushed with the toe points but nobody wore crampons while climbing the ridge and there wasn't time now to put them on. With an outstretched arm he could almost reach the other side with his ice axe.

He tried to dig his toes gently into snow so he could push forward. The snow bridge might collapse if he kicked. He needed to move fifteen to twenty inches to get a secure anchor on the top of the block. As he reached out he heard a gun shot. A bullet ricocheted off the rocks they had just descended.

"Hurry, Boss. Somebody is shooting and you're a sitting duck stretched out like that," Juan yelled. "He is a lousy shot but why take chances. I am letting out a little extra slack and moving inside the tunnel a little further. Another wild shot might come up here."

Roy pushed the snow with his toes and his left hand jamming his ice axe down on the top of the block as the bridge collapsed. He swung like a pendulum into the face of the block and he hung on with his right hand. His toes dug into the wall and he started to climb up. He lifted his left hand to the top of the wall, reached over to the flat surface and scratched a handhold.

A deafening explosion blasted the ice block out of the V- shaped gully one hundred fifty feet above them on the right side. Tons of ice, rocks and snow cascaded down onto the slope above the ramp. The avalanche swept down onto the ramp burying the opening to the tunnel and forcing the block that Tom lay on to add to the material avalanching down to the next terrace three hundred feet below.

Roy was aware that some time had passed. He was hanging from the rope under the overhanging edge of the ramp. The block he had just crossed over to was gone and there was nothing below him but space. "Juan," he yelled, "Throw me another line."

There was no answer.

"Juan, can you hear me?" Roy sensed that he had been hit by some rocks or chunks of ice. His left arm was numb and blood dripped from his fingers. His left leg hurt below the knee and his right shoulder ached when he tried to move his right arm. The ice axe hung from the wrist loop on his right arm. "Juan, I am okay if you can hear me. Bruised a little, some cuts but I don't think anything is broken."

The only sounds were the waterfalls above and the clatter of rocks bouncing down the cliffs above and toward the east. The sound of the explosion and the thunder of the avalanche had dissipated before Roy had regained consciousness.

The first chunks of the avalanche had knocked him out. He had fallen off the block had dropped more than twenty feet down the face. The rope sliced into the overhang pulling him underneath it. The avalanche had swept over him pushing the block Tom had been on off the cliff.

He hung there in his harness for a few minutes gathering his thoughts. Anger was setting and he felt the adrenaline pushing away the pain. He set his jumars and inched his way up the rope to the ceiling of snow above him. With his ice axe he burrowed a hole up through the snow. The snow lip was two feet thick where he emerged.

There was no slack in the rope. Six feet from his hole, the rope disappeared into a solid wall of snow. The opening to the tunnel had been buried. He tried to pull the rope out but it was stuck tight. Juan and the remaining seven staff from Wallace Images had been buried alive.

Roy dug frantically with his fingers and the ice axe trying to follow the rope back toward the opening of the tunnel. After clawing and digging for an hour he finally collapsed from exhaustion. He had tunneled in only five to six feet. The rope would not budge from its icy grip. The Adrenaline rush wore off, the pain returned and exhaustion left him too tired to accept or reject the death of his closest friend and the others. They just weren't there anymore.

For a moment nothing existed. Roy saw himself lying there. "Roy, you have to get up. Start walking. Start climbing down. I'll guide you." Roy sensed a voice, his own voice, detached from his battered body sitting in the snow.

More than once over the years he found himself seemingly detached from his body. He had watched himself lecturing to his students at the university.

He could sit in the back rows of the auditorium or float above and still speak to himself at the podium, directing the lecture. At other times, this presence would assemble diagrams and abstract ideas and intuitions and project them like a floating map in front of him to study.

This inner being could display and trace through thousands of program objects to find an inverted probability in a decision model. Roy had found that at times, when he was prepared, he could he could consciously and deliberately tap this subconscious awareness. Now the voice was speaking to him for its own survival.

"Roy, cut the rope as close to the wall as you can. You might need a thirty-foot length of rope."

"Now cross to the east side of the terrace. I'll follow."

"When we come to the rock wall there will be a series of rock ledges you can climb down."

"Take your time. It will be okay. You can do it."
"Don't look back. There is nothing to see."

For twenty minutes Roy mechanically climbed down the rock face detached from his usual mental processes. There was no sensation in his fingers. He saw his hands grasping small ledges and his feet reaching for small footholds. The space below him had no significance. His body was climbing down. His eyes caught movement on the glacier far below. A lone figure had already descended the two lower terraces and was walking on the surface of the South Crillon glacier.

Roy slowly began to focus on what he was doing. A sudden sense of urgency overwhelmed him. . He was anxious to get down off the cliff, travel the length of the second terrace and the first terrace and find the route to the Crillion glacier. He was driven to catch the person who had killed his friend. He wanted that person to know pain. His guide retreated. He seemed alone again.

The second terrace was relatively smooth. He jogged and jumped the smaller crevasses. At the bottom edge of the terrace he could see further down the South Crillion glacier. It would take another hour to get to it. He could also see a second figure descending onto the glacier below. A faint dust cloud rose from the rolling rocks dislodged by the person as he reached the bottom of the ridge bordering the first terrace. Roy wondered why the two were so far apart.

The sun was low on the western horizon when Roy finally descended onto the South Crillion glacier. The mountains on the western edge of the glacier blocked the sun. It was getting colder. Roy had his ice axe, a short piece of rope, a pocketknife and the radio in his pocket. He had taken off his pack before attempting to reach Tom's body.

It would be a few more hours before he could attempt a transmission. If he traveled too far down the glacier and followed it after it turned north, the high mountain ridge on his right might block the satellite access. He started down the glacier in pursuit of the two people ahead of him. Would they wait to ambush him somewhere in the crevasses and moraines covering the glacier?

The lower reaches of the South Crillon exhibited all the signs of an old receding glacier. It was covered with mounds of dirt and rock twenty feet high. Every inch of glacier was either covered by a veneer of dirt and rocks or pocked with small rocks that had melted into the ice through the warming action of the sun. No sound of the others came from the glacier below.

He picked his way through the boulders and hummocks of rock- covered ice. For two hours the only sounds were of his breathing and of his ice axe hitting rocks. He had lost his crampons in the avalanche and footing on some icy sections was treacherous. In the dim twilight he found crampon tracks in the ice. Small pockets of clean ice pushed up when the spikes of the crampons dug into the glacier's surface. The tracks were microscopic in the vastness of the glacier but distinctive. The others were travelling toward the north side of the glacier to shorten the travel distance as the glacier made a sweeping turn north.

There was a time, years before, when he wandered these rock piles leisurely taking samples. Picking rocks up, striking them with a hammer, smelling the fractures, looking at the crystalline structure of the exposed rock with a magnifying glass.

A small groan reached up from deep in the earth. Hundreds of small dirt and snow avalanches could be heard cascading from the ridges and slopes above. It was a small earthquake.

The elasticity of the ice absorbed the vibrations. Roy continued as fast as he could. How many earthquakes are there in a year up here? He remembered recording four a day for two months after a big quake in 1958. Was this one a precursor to another big one or the aftermath of one he hadn't felt?

The glacier valley narrowed and descended steeply. The ice turned into a small icefall that looked like a photograph of rapids in a river. The ice didn't splash like a river but pushed up until it fell over in a jumbled, unstable pile.

The turbulence through this section removed any danger from hidden crevasses. The primary danger was from large blocks of ice falling over. The melted water from the warm days lubricated the base of the glacier. Its movement increased toward the end of the day and into the twilight. It was more stable in the morning hours.

In a few places he found that the others had used the toe points of their crampons to climb small, near vertical walls. He knew he was losing time whenever he had to find a way around the obstacle that the others had simply clambered. over

He reached a point where a solid coastal mountain ridge divided the glacier. Part of the glacier flowed south and the rest moved north. Beyond the ridge was the ocean. The southern flow sent ice blocks into Lake Crillon. The northern flow dropped ice into the Crillon Inlet at the head of Lituya Bay.

It had been near dark for some time. Roy knew he had only one more chance at a transmission for several hours. The eastern ridge would be in the way of the satellite orbit. Once he moved down the glacier a mile or two more there was another glacier descending from the east that would open the horizon for viewing.

He stopped and sat down. He suddenly realized how tired he was. He fumbled with the transmitter. "Hello Watcher. Do you copy?"

"Roy." The speaker at the other end didn't bother to deal with preliminary code exchanges. "We have been worried since you missed your last transmission. We found the helicopter. The pilot and passenger's throats had been cut."

"Out." Roy said weakly. He didn't bother to respond. "They will find me," he said aloud. "So," he thought, "Kurt killed the crew when he climbed up to the helicopter. Why? He must be working with Eugene?"

Roy fell asleep on the dirt-covered ice.

He woke up with a start. Something had shaken him. The clattering sound of rocks told him there had been another small earthquake.

The black silhouette of the eastern peaks and ridges against an opaque sky was the first hint of morning.

The sky to the west was filled with stars but otherwise was black. How much time had he lost? His back was stiff and cold, he was hungry and thirsty. The pockets of water on the glacier had frozen. Even the flow of the small surface streams had been suspended.

He found a few tracks. They became more elusive on the flatter section of the stagnating glacier. The tracks continued toward the north, toward Lituya Bay where fishing boats sometimes entered to get ice for their holds to keep their catch of fish preserved. If there was a boat in the bay, Kurt and Eugene would escape.

What kind of people are these who would kill a whole group of people? Why did they do it? If they would kill so easily they certainly wouldn't hesitate to kill him or the crew on a fishing boat. They had guns and all he had was a pocket knife, thirty feet of perlon cord and an ice axe. Possibly he had an element of surprise if they thought he had been killed in the avalanche with the others.

The dirt slopes above the north side of the glacier rose three hundred feet at the maximum possible angle, the angle of repose. Any steeper and the material rolls down. Above the dirt slopes a forest grew, carpeting the side of the mountain above up to an altitude of two thousand feet. Above that the slopes rounded off and were covered with clumps of grass and low bushes that could survive being buried in snow for half the year. There wasn't enough vegetation on the upper slopes to provide the nutrients to feed a forest.

Roy traveled around the shoulder of the ridge that formed the north side of the glacier and saw the jumbled mess of the moraine of another glacier descending onto the one he was walking on. The North Crillon glacier descended from the upper reaches of a valley parallel to the South Crillon glacier. The two merged and descended into the inlet sending a continuous stream of icebergs into Lituya bay. The entrance to the bay was too narrow to let the larger ice blocks access to the ocean.

He moved left around the convergence and headed for the forest that grew along the western slope. There were a number of streams running on the surface of the glacier and along the edge of the glacier. The stream flow noise covered the sound of his ice axe and of hisfeet on the rocks. The noise would also cover any sounds the others might make.

The brush was thick near the water. There, under the canopy of the Douglas fir, the ground was covered with a thick carpet of moss.

Huckleberry bushes were stunted but were covered with white berries still waiting to ripen, turning purple.

The sky was bright even though the sun had not risen high enough to shine onto the eastern end of the bay. Through the trees Roy could see a small fishing boat in the Inlet. Two men in a small dinghy were rowing toward the shore.

Roy couldn't yet see the beach or who was standing there as he ran quietly on the moss. The brush grew denser as he approached the beach. The mosquitoes were swarming.

Two shots shattered the quiet air. Seagulls screamed and rose off the water. Roy pushed a branch aside and saw Eugene and Kurt standing next to the bodies of two fishermen. Each had a gun in his hand, looking at each other. Eugene, closest to Roy, was walking slowly toward Kurt. Kurt dropped his gun onto rocks near his feet.

Roy tried to move closer to get a better view and stepped on a branch under the moss. Kurt heard the slight sound and saw Roy.

"Roy, watch out!" Kurt yelled. "This guy is a killer. Run."

The sound of the gun firing and the sound of the branch next to Roy's head breaking were simultaneous.

"Hold it," Eugene said. "Come over here slowly." He backed up slowly so that he could keep Kurt and Roy in view. "Drop the stick. It's no match for a 45."

"So, you two work together." Eugene seemed to be putting a puzzle together.

"What do you mean?" Roy asked. "It looks like you two murderers are working together."

"Roy," Kurt said. "he can't get us both."

"Want to bet?" Eugene motioned Roy to move toward Kurt. "I've been tracking you two for two years now."

"What the hell are you talking about?" Roy bristled.

"This outdoor gimmick for transferring top secret data and design information was clever. Was Juan in on it?"

"I still don't know what you are talking about. Who are you anyway? I figured you worked with Kurt. The chopper you heard two days ago was military. It had searched the site of the crash that Kurt and I had gone to. Kurt, it appears, had cut the throats of the pilot and crew and smashed the radio. He told me they had died in the crash."

Roy turned toward Kurt. "That chopper was working with you, right?"

"You figured that out, did you?" Kurt responded to Roy but kept his eyes fixed on Eugene.

The mosquitoes were swarming. Eugene started to brush some off his face and Kurt lunged at him. He partially slipped on the rocks as Eugene fired. Kurt fell grabbing his left arm.

Eugene quickly pointed the pistol at Roy to make sure he didn't move, then returned the aim to Kurt. Eugene stepped over to where Kurt had dropped his pistol.

Roy said, "Eugene, Brad suggested you were CIA. If that is the case you can verify that I am not working with Kurt."

"I'm not CIA. Used to be. Raymond Wallace hired me to find out who was leaking secrets."

"Who was it?"

"Looks like it was Dr. Gilmore," Eugene responded. He stooped, picked the pistol up out of the water, pointed it at Kurt and pulled the trigger. Kurt smiled. Eugene threw the empty gun into deeper water.

"Listen, Eugene," Roy said, "in my pocket is a transmitter that you can use to contact General Davis. He can vouch for who I am. It is line-of-sight to the XCOM satellite. The mountain there blocks your transmission. You will have to go back up the glacier to the intersection of the North and South Crillion glacier."

"Take your parka off and throw it over here... slowly." Eugene backed up slightly. Kurt was still sitting on the wet rocks holding his arm.

Roy took off the parka and tossed it toward Eugene. "Check the inside cargo pocket. Left side."

Eugene squatted, keeping a focus on Kurt while he fished the radio out of the parka. "Looks familiar," he said. "How did you get it?"

"I test equipment for General Davis. Juan doesn't... didn't, know about this side of my activities."

Roy looked at Kurt. "Why did you kill Raymond Wallace?" Eugene looked at Roy, "Wasn't that an accident?"

"No. Kurt poured water around the outside of the tarp, which froze and cut off the oxygen supply. I guess Raymond figured out who Kurt was."

"How about Ralph? Did Kurt kill him or did Todd?"

"Neither. Marcy did. If she hadn't, Kurt would have. He found out that Ralph had recognized him as one of the leaders on an XYCore trip last year just before they had a security breach. Ralph had told Tom, not knowing that Tom was working with Kurt. Ralph also made a note in his diary that he had told Tom. Kurt most likely set her up to do it. She had confided in him why she was working at Wallace Images."

"She was in the crevasse!"

"She lowered herself in. She knew somebody would come looking and find her."

"Why?"

"Revenge. She found out it was Ralph who had raped her sister."

"How about Brad? Was his death an accident or was he murdered?"

"Tom did that." Roy looked at Kurt. "Did you put him up to it?"

Kurt didn't answer the question. "You guys going to let me bleed to death?"

"Not a bad idea," Eugene said. "What about Brad?"

"I guess Kurt and Tom got nervous about Brad spending too much time with me. Tom knew that Brad knew a lot about everybody's past and figured he was bending under the strain of the trip."

"Okay," Eugene said. "What do we do now?"

"You are going to have to trust me. My thought is you need to go up the glacier and call the General. Have him get down here.

Second, I want to get out to that boat and use their radio. I might have to take it toward the mouth of the bay to get a good signal out."

"What about Kurt?"

"I guess you are going to have to trust me some more and let me have the gun. I'll take him with me out to the boat."

Kurt smiled. "Good work, Roy. Now we can get out of here."

Roy looked at Kurt. "You killed my closest friend up there. My first instinct is to shoot you now but I know some other people who want to talk to you."

Eugene looked at Roy for a few seconds before handing him the pistol. The ground shook slightly; some rocks could be heard bouncing off the cliffs at the head of Lituya Bay. A series of waves rippled through the water, an iceberg to calve off from the glacier jutting into the inlet.

Roy pointed the gun at Kurt. "Into the boat. Keep the oars in the locks. If one even slips, I'll shoot." Roy helped by Eugene pushed the boat into the water. Roy stepped in carefully, watching Kurt. Kurt was waiting for a mistake that he could take advantage of. Roy watched for an aggressive move by Kurt.

Eugene disappeared into the underbrush as he headed up the hill toward the West Side of the glacier.

Kurt rowed slowly. His injured arm seemed to have recovered from the flesh wound.

Roy's mind raced over the past two weeks. Kurt had spent a lot of time with Tom playing chess, with standard pieces. "How did Tom pass information to you?"

"You'll have to ask him," Kurt answered.

"I figure it was in the chess pieces that disappeared. The helicopter we heard was picking up the pieces you left with the bodies.

We went to the helicopter crash site, not to rescue people but for you to retrieve chess pieces they had picked up."

They reached the fishing boat, The Galavanter out of Anchorage. Roy had Kurt maneuver the stern up to the side. Roy backed out of the dinghy and onto the deck and then motioned for Kurt to climb aboard and sit on the deck next to the net drum.

He could watch Kurt as he started the engine and anchor hoist. The diesel engine blew smoke into the air when the anchor was up. Roy turned the bow toward the opening of the bay. There were a number of small icebergs drifting in the bay. Roy kept the throttle down and had to quickly glance at the water in front of him while he kept an eye on Kurt. It was four miles to the mouth of the Bay. They passed the south side of Cenotaph Island, scarred by mysterious waves that washed away parts of the forest. Seagulls swooped down waiting for a fisherman to throw a fish head or fish guts into the water.

The Galavanter's bow sent out waves that washed over the shelves of the icebergs they passed. Roy braced his right hip against the wheel. He reached for the radio with his left hand and held the gun in his right hand.

"Breaker, breaker. This is the Galavanter. This is the Galavanter."

"Breaker, breaker. This is an emergency. The crew as been shot. The crew is dead. The Galavanter is in Lituya Bay."

There was the whistling squawk of a signal finding its way through the circuitry and an answer. "Galavanter, this is the Iskum. Say again."

"Iskum, this is the Galavanter. The crew has been shot. Treat the people on board as hostile until clarified." Roy didn't want to give any chance of Kurt escaping even if he had to be held until authorities arrived. "Call the Coast Guard. Rendezvous outside Lituya bay. Copy?"

"Galavanter. This is the Iskum. Will contact Coast Guard. Who are you?"

"Iskum. My name is Roy..."

The Galavanter bumped into a floating block of ice and lurched to the left. Roy lost his balance and his hip came off the wheel. The wheel spun rapidly as the boat slid off the small ledge of ice.

Kurt struck like a rattlesnake. He had been waiting for the slightest break in Roy's concentration to attack. He moved as if he had rehearsed his motions in his mind. He sprang toward Roy, grabbing a gaff pole used to hook the larger fish in the gills as they were being pulled onto the boat. Kurt jabbed at Roy with the sharp three-inch hook at the end of the three-foot shaft.

The gaff caught Roy's shirt and gave Roy a chance to kick Kurt's injured arm. The gaff fell to the side. Kurt lunged at Roy and knocked him to the deck. Kurt grasped an axe clamped to the wall of the cabin, raiseding it to take a hard swing at Roy.

CHAPTER 15
SHAKEDOWN

It started with a slight groan. It came from deep, inside the earth. The earth's crust along a fault line east of Lituya bay shifted slightly, sending vibrations through the peaks and glaciers. The vibration knocked loose rocks from the cliffs and ledges triggering avalanches of rocks and raising dust clouds that filled the valleys. Unsettled snow avalanched and the tilting towers of ice in the icefalls of the descending glaciers toppled and crunched into the crevasses below them.

Tables in the Red Dog Saloon in Juneau, one hundred miles to the southeast, quivered then rocked back and forth. The chandeliers swayed, women screamed. The rustic swinging doors of the western style entrance to the tavern flapped back and forth as patrons rushed into the street. A number of them rushed back in to get their drinks, then returned to the street. Telephone poles whipped back and forth like metronomes

Large chunks of ice at the end of the glacier forming the back end of Lake Crillon broke away and slid into the water. The calved icebergs displaced the water. Then buoyed by the pressure of water, they rose up and settled down creating deep waves which moved westward.

Seconds later the fabric of the earth's crust ripped open. The west side of the fault jolted south another twelve feet. The seismic reading would be 8.2 on the Richter scale.

Southeastern Alaska was shaken. The tops of ridges cascaded downward. Rivers of rock flowed off the slopes onto the glaciers, filling in crevasses and moving forward for distances of as much as a quarter of a mile. Glacial valleys were filled with clouds of dust that would settle onto the snow and provide a time mark. Glaciers moved several feet excavating walls, of ice 500 feet and dropping them down the slopes into the glacial valleys below.

Eugene had reached a broad grassy knoll above the junction of the two glaciers where he would have line-of-sight transmission to the satellite. He was standing looking east up the North Crillon glacier. As he pushed the transmission button the ground lurched violently and he fell. He tried to stand and was thrown to the ground again. He landed on one knee.

A blast of acrid smelling dust knocked him down. He hesitated to breathe and pulled his shirt over his mouth before inhaling. The ground heaved a fourth time and settled.

Eugene looked up the glacier and saw torrents of rock cascading down both sides toward the center.

Instinct told him to run but he had no idea to where. He looked at his pack. It had moved twelve feet. The ground in front of him had split carrying his pack north.

From the north came a sound he could not imagine. Adrenaline pushed the real world into slow motion. The western slope of the mountain at the head end of Lituya Bay was cascading into the narrow inlets formed by the Crillon and LaPerouse glaciers, displacing all the water and forcing it upward. The water crashed down filling the void it had made, compressing hundred of cubic yards of air. The compressed air exploded, blowing the water upward like a giant geyser.

The splash generated a wall of water with unimaginably destructive force. Water raced up and over the shoulder of the ridge across the northern branch of the bay. Every tree in the forest on the ridge was ripped from the slopes along with all the soil. The shoulder was scoured clean to an altitude of 1,800 feet.

The wall of water moved south across the bay stripping Cenotaph Island of its vegetation. The surge of water mixed with an entire forest smashed into the shoreline, raced five hundred feet up the southern slopes of the bay, then turned west toward the ocean.

The forest of the southern slope became part of the slurry of ice, dirt and trees that washed back into the bay. A two-hundred-foot tidal wave of debris surged in the direction of the "Galavanter" on its way toward the forested spit that protected the bay from the ravages of the ocean.

Farther north a portion of Kodiak Island would sink. A Tsunami warning would be issued for the Aleutians, Hawaii and Japan. The seismic reading of 8.2 was high but the epicenter was 100 miles from the nearest town.

The fishing boat at the northern inlet of the bay disappeared in the destruction of the initial thundering splash. The "Galavanter," now three miles from the source of the wave was hurtled upward by the leading edge of the wave after it swept off the southern slope.

Kurt was swinging an axe at Roy when the boat was lifted and pitched forward. He fell, dropping the axe as he grabbed a line on the rigging mast in front of the wheelhouse. Roy grabbed the railing on the wheelhouse as the bow of the "Galavanter" nosed down the wave.

The face of the wave was steep enough to allow the "Galavanter" to slide down the front of it as it moved toward the ocean. The "Galavanter" was *surfing* the biggest waves in the world! They crested over the thin line of forest at the entrance to the bay. Roy and Kurt looked down fifty feet onto the tops of seventy to hundred foot high trees as the "Galavanter" was swept over the barrier toward the Pacific Ocean.

The crew of the "Iskum" half a mile out in the ocean watched the "Galavanter" riding down the wall of water. When the wave reached deep water it rushed forward and dropped the "Galavanter." The crew of the "Iskum" lost sight of the "Galavanter" as the wave bore down, then swept under them.

When the wave passed they saw the shattered remains of the "Galavanter," which had first crashed on ground when the wave entered deep water, then was lifted by the ocean returning to it normal level. Kurt and Roy had been slammed into unconsciousness and were floating among the debris of the boat. The "Iskum" was maneuvered close enough for the crew to hook the clothing of Roy and Kurt with a pike pole, dragging them close enough to pull them into the boat.

The crew expected the two to be dead. Kurt coughed. A crew member grabbed Roy's wrist to find a pulse and put an ear on Roy's chest. "This one is alive, but out cold."

Kurt dragged himself to his hands and knees and managed to stand. "That man is a terrorist. He killed the crew of the "Galavanter" and four people in my camping party. If you are not careful he will kill us too. You had better tie him up." Kurt passed out.

Eugene wondered how he had survived and was screaming into the radio. "Mayday, Mayday, Mayday...get me the General"

"This is the Gabby..." a calm voice came over the radio.

"Somebody just nuked us."

"Say again."

"I'm calling for Roy Graham. The god dam earth is coming apart up here."

"Relax. Where is Roy?"

"He is on a fishing boat with a madman name Kurt Rail. Kurt has killed eleven people. I think the boat they are on just got destroyed by a giant tidal wave."

"Who are you?"

"Eugene..."

"Relax, Commander Langley, support is arriving."

"How do you know who I am?"

"What is your position?" the voice asked

"At the terminus of the North Crillon glacier."

Seconds later a helicopter could be heard coming down the glacier.

CHAPTER 16
ESCAPES

Roy felt the vibration of the diesel engine before he opened his eyes. His first thoughts were a vague recollection of the boat he was on before it crashed. He drifted in and out of consciousness. Some kind of dream. Panic welled up as his dream flashed a battle scene where Kurt was swinging an axe at him.

The smell of diesel and the throbbing of the boat's engine pushed the dream away. He was awake. He tried to move then realized his arms were tied behind him and his legs were bound. He was lying on his stomach on top a pile of ropes and chains on a boat.

It took several seconds before Roy could recall that the boat he had been on was suddenly in the air and then falling. He closed his eyes and tried to determine if he was injured. He stepped through a self-assessment protocol

"Tighten your foot muscles," he thought. "Relax."

"No pain. Good."

"Tense the knees."

"Hold it."

"Relax."

"Hurts but nothing feels broken."

He tensed and relaxed his stomach, back, arms and neck. Everything seemed to ache but nothing felt broken.

Judging by the sound of the engine and the water hitting the hull he was in the forward storage area of a small boat. This must be the "Iskum," he thought. He opened his eyes. It was nearly dark. Two dirty portholes let enough light in for him to see.

Had Kurt survived the crash of the "Galavanter"? If so, where was he? Roy looked around as best he could. He was alone. He rolled over and sat up with his wrists pushing against a rusty chain. He rubbed the ropes on the chain. The pitching and yawing of the boat and the smell of diesel fumes and fish clouded his senses. His only thought was of the chain nicking the rope and breaking a strand, then another strand and another. When the rope finally weakened enough for him to free his hands he started thinking about what to do next.

The door into the engine room was latched from the other side. There were piles of rope, nets, a tank of acetylene, some fishing gaffs, boxes of cork floats, reels of line the thickness of net line, shackles for connecting lines, fuel cans and a variety of other items that might be needed but would be in the way anyplace else. He found that there was an overhead hatch that opened onto the forward deck. There probably was a small overturned skiff above it. He push gently, then harder. Nothing moved. Running his hand around the perimeter of the hatch he found it was latched from the inside. Slipping the latch he lifted the cover a fraction of an inch; just enough to peer out. There was a skiff over the hatch. Feet went past. He could hear a slight scuffle and heard Kurt's voice.

"Move your ass to the stern or I'll feed you to the fish," Kurt said. "Give me any trouble, and I'll shoot the kid first."

The feet moved to the back of the boat.

"How many people on the boat?" Roy wondered. He heard a ruckus coming noise from the stern over the noise of the engine. It sounded like Kurt was smashing the radio and other instruments.

He opened the hatch cover enough to let air in and put a piece of cork under the lip to hold it up. IIe wanted some fresh air but not so much movement as to catch someone's attention. At least not immediately.

He remembered the time his dad, a tug boat captain, was marooned in the middle of Puget Sound while towing a large raft of logs. The valve on an acetylene bottle left unsecured by the previous crew was knocked open as the bottle rolled around. The acetylene filled the engine chamber and the engine stalled from the lack of oxygen. His dad opened the hatch to the engine room and realized what had happened. He held his breath, climbed into the hold, opened the portholes and went top side to wait until the gas had cleared out. Had he been smoking when he opened the hatch or had he tried to start the engine, the boat would have exploded.

"Okay dad, lets try it again," he thought. "I hope nobody smokes."

Roy found the hose for the acetylene torch, then rummaged though the boxes and found a knife. He cut the torch coupling off the hose and slipped the hose under the door into the engine room. He opened the valve on the bottled gas.

He opened the hatch and slid if off the deck frame so he could climb out.

The acetylene filled the engine room. The engine sputtered once or twice before it quit. Kurt was ready to shoot one of the crew when the engine died. He waved the gun at the deckhand and pointed to the engine room. "Go find out what the problem is," he said, pushing him into the door leading to the engine room. The crew member opened the door and the odor of acetylene filled the air.

The owner of the boat said, "It'll blow," and headed for the stern railing. The others started to follow him. Kurt knew that if he shot anyone the flash from the gun would ignite the gas. He threw a knife into the back of the owner's leg. "Stick around," he said.

Kurt snarled at the deckhand ordering him to go down and open the portholes to let the gas clear out and find out where it came from. Turning to the owner, he asked, "Where is the other guy? Did you fish him out of the water?"

The owner of the "Iskum" said the other fellow was tied up in the storage area ahead of the engine room. Kurt then suspected that Roy had had something to do with the engine stalling. He yelled down to the deckhand to bring Roy out.

The crew member asked if he could wait until the gas cleared.

Kurt commanded, "Hold your breath. Bring that son-of-bitch out here."

Robby Simpson, climbed down into the engine room, opened a porthole and stuck his face out to get a breath of fresh air. He groped his way forward to the storage area, unlatched the door and opened it. Robby saw the gas bottle and closed the valve. "The hatch is open. He's gone," Robby yelled back to Kurt. He grabbed the ropes that Roy had cut through and worked his way aft past the engine. He ran the few steps to the opening to the deck gasping to get some fresh air.

Kurt stuck the gun in his face and said, "Where's Roy?"

"He is not there. The hatch is opened. He must have climbed out."

Robby offered the cut rope to Kurt. Kurt snatched it and whipped it across Robby's face.

"Get up here. Go back with the others."

The owner, holding his leg sat on the stern railing. The knife was still imbedded. His twelve-year-son stood next to him. Robby walked back to them and turned around to face Kurt. Kurt stood with his back to the engine room opening and aimed the pistol at the twelve-year-old.

"Roy," he shouted, "I know you're out there. I am going to count to five and then shoot the kid. One...two..."

Roy hadn't climbed out through the hatch but had buried himself under the ropes and chains. Robby had stood on Roy's hand when he was looking up through the hatch. When Robby left, Roy crawled out from his cover and grabbed a five-foot fishing gaff, a pole with a three-inch hook on the end. He moved quietly to the side of the opening to the deck. He saw the three at the railing and signaled for them not to indicate he was there.

Three were surprised to see Roy. Their eyes grew wider as Kurt said "Four." He knew their eyes were opening at the prospect of dying as he was squeezing the trigger.

Roy shoved the pole between Kurt's legs, raised it so the point of the hook was up and facing Kurt's crotch and pulled back as hard as he could. The gun went off wildly as Roy pulled Kurt into the engine room on the gaff. Kurt's feet were pulled off the deck by the jerk of the gaff and his face hit the top step as he crashed into the engine room. The twelve-year-old threw up. Robby rushed to the opening to see what happened to Kurt. He picked the gun up from off the deck and looked in as Roy reset the gaff and pulled up a second time.

Roy saw Robby looking at him. "That second one was for me," Roy said.

"Is he dead?"

"I hope not," Roy smiled. "Let's get him up top."

"How do I know you won't try to kill us like he did?" Robby asked.

"Somebody said you guys were hostile."

"Okay," Roy said, "keep the gun on me while I get him onto the deck. With luck the Coast Guard will be along in a little while. I'll sit over there and you can shoot me if and when you want. In the meantime why don't you let me take the knife out of the skipper."

Roy set the gaff aside and went over to the owner. He looked him in the eye and started to say "Hi, my name is Roy,." and jerked the knife out without warning of his intention to do so. It happened so fast the owner just stared at him and then sagged onto the deck.

Roy threw the knife overboard and walked back to where Kurt was lying. He rolled Kurt over and rummaged through his pockets. Kurt was wearing a belt inside his pants with a pouch in it like a money belt. The gaff had ripped through the belt and punched a hole in a plastic package. Inside the package were the two kings from Tom's chess set. Roy put the package in his pants pocket and rolled Kurt back onto his stomach.

"Can I hoist him up by the feet like a large fish and have my picture taken?" Roy asked, then sat down on a capstan. He reached for the gaff and said, "Kurt, if you move, I'll feed your guts to the fish." He set the point of the gaff on Kurt's hip.

Robby said, "No, but I'll hoist a distress flag." He pulled a fluorescent pink flag from a box next to the engine room and raised it up the mast.

Everyone grew silent. The boat floundered in the waves and swells. Water slapped against the hull. Seagulls circled the "Iskum" screaming at each other, waiting for a scrap of food. Usually people don't sit on the deck doing nothing unless they are eating lunch.

A Coast Guard Search and Rescue plane flew over, circled, dipped it's wings and climbed higher but continued to circle. A helicopter could be heard coming from the direction of Lituya bay. The "Iskum" had been drifting south in the offshore current and was now surrounded by large chunks of ice, thousands of trees that had been stripped of their bark and fish that had been killed in the explosive force of the wave. The helicopter had pontoons but the pilot had difficulty finding a place to land because of the debris.

The helicopter flew to the shore and landed. The pilot used a flashlight to signal in Morse code that a larger Coast Guard cutter was coming. It might be an hour's wait. They again waited.

A loud burping horn sounded three times. They saw a large white vessel with an orange diagonal stripe on its bow pushing gently through the debris toward them. Roy said, "There are enough logs out there that we could probably walk out and meet them. I'll bet this mess screws up fishing for a long time."

The crew, Kurt and Roy were taken aboard the Coast Guard ship. The captain was apprised of the need to keep Kurt under surveillance. He indicated he had already been briefed and understood the circumstances.

The helicopter took off from the shore and landed on the helicopter pad of the vessel. Roy climbed in. "Hi, General. Good to see you again." Roy gave General Parker, his long time friend, a mock salute.

"Hi, Roy," Eugene called to him from a seat in the rear of the helicopter.

Roy turned around and gave Eugene a thumbs up sign. The helicopter lifted off.

General Parker said, "You have got to see this. It looks like an atomic bomb went off in here."

The helicopter flew north along and just off the beach until it reached the mouth of Lituya Bay. The pilot hovered so Roy could study the ragged remains of the spit separating the bay from the ocean.

"We rode over that on a fishing boat," he said, "and lived to tell about it."

The pilot lifted the craft higher so that the bay was in full view. Logs and ice covered the surface. The shore was covered with logs stacked and scattered like a dropped box of tooth picks. A thin grey cloud covered the bay at an altitude of 1,000 feet.

As they neared the head end of the bay the destructive force of the wave became more apparent. The mountain ridge forming the western slope of Gilbert inlet was stripped of all vegetation to an altitude of 1,800 feet. It was nothing but barren rock.

"If we go south I can show you the fault line," Eugene said. "I was practically standing on it."

The pilot flew to where he had picked Eugene up and landed. Roy got out and looked, walked a few yards along the fault and returned.

"Let's go up to where the rest of the party was lost." He pointed south. "Take a left at the next glacier. Follow it up to the saddle between two peaks. There will be a glacier on the right. Follow it."

The pilot flew up the glacier, staying two hundred feet above the ice. Roy tried to trace the path he had taken while following Kurt down the glacier.

"Eugene," Roy shouted back over the noise of the engines, "how did you follow Kurt."

"Carefully. I think he knew I was behind him but didn't seem concerned. He traveled fairly fast. I had trouble keeping up. The sound of his crampons and ice axe hitting rocks made it easy to follow even though I couldn't see him."

Roy pointed to some of the large rock avalanche tracks that had swept off the slopes and covered the glacier. "The mother of mother lodes has probably been uncovered and nobody knows it," he said to the General. If we had more time it would be fun to explore."

"There," Roy signaled the pilot to turn left and climb. He said, "go up to the rock ridge separating the glacier from the snowfield above."

"There is somebody down there," the General said pointing to a patch of snow between two large avalanche tracks and the base of the ridge. The pilot circled several times looking for a spot flat enough to land. He finally had to descend off the steep section and land half-a-mile down the slope.

Roy and Eugene got out of the helicopter. There was an extra ice axe and rope which Roy took. He started running up the slope, tying the rope around his waist as he moved. Eugene followed. Roy could tell that he had been banged up more than he thought when the "Galavanter" crashed. He thought, "It doesn't hurt if you're dead." He could see Juan's red parka. Nobody was moving. They were sitting in a circle around a boiling pot of water.

Roy was breathing hard when he reached the circle. Juan looked up, smiled and asked, "Coffee or hot chocolate?" Then he and the others stood. They all said, "What took you so long, Boss?" and laughed.

Roy looked at them for a while and asked, "How did you survive? I saw you get buried in the avalanche Kurt started. Where is Grant?"

Juan shook his head. "He didn't make it."

Eugene came up behind Roy. "When I saw you go to Tom's body on the edge of the crevasse I knew that Kurt was setting a trap. He was ready to push the boulder to start the avalanche. I fired a warning shot."

"So that was the gunshot we heard," Michael said. "I thought somebody was shooting at us."

"We scrambled into the tunnel that went to the base of the cliff," Harry explained, "just before the avalanche covered the opening. Juan was belaying you and was buried. We were able to dig him out but your rope just disappeared into the wall of ice. We tried digging out but couldn't."

Juan said, "Marcy and Todd used their flashlights and followed the tunnel uphill. They thought there might be an opening."

"We followed the tunnel for half an hour," Marcy said. "It was slow going because the tunnel was the bed of an under-glacier river. There wasn't any water in it because an avalanche had covered the opening at the top. We didn't know what to do."

"It was like being in an ice tomb," Todd remembered. "Most of use got into our sleeping bags to stay warm. We took turns at trying to dig up through the softer snow and ice. After three hours, I think we gave up."

James said, "It turned out to be more than thirty five feet thick. We never would have made it."

"What do you mean," the General said, as he finished climbing up the slope from the helicopter, "you never would have made it? You're here. You got out"

"I think we all prayed or something," Juan said. "Nothing left to do? Then boom."

"Boom?" Roy asked.

"This big mother. earth started shaking something fierce. I thought we were goners for sure." Juan smiled and shook his head. "I thought we were goners."

James said, "It must have been a big earthquake. The ceiling of the tunnel collapsed and buried Grant. He was digging. The ice block that fell on him was more than thirty feet thick. It happened so fast. The rest of us were next to the side wall and the ceiling missed us when it fell. When everything quieted down, we were looking at blue sky."

"There were avalanches roaring down all over the place," Ian said. "I have no idea how we survived. Roy, how did you get out?"

Roy said, "Lets tell our adventure stories around some good food and drinks later. For the moment let's get out of here."

A second helicopter could be heard coming up the glacier. "I ordered some more transportation," General Parker said. "Do you guys want to get out of here?"

On the way down to the helicopter James asked Roy if they could get some of the singing ice he had mentioned at the beginning of the trip.

"General," Roy shouted over the engine noise, "have the second chopper meet us in Juneau. James, Eugene and I should go and get Raymond Wallace and Ralph Dresner. We are also going to detour and get some ice from Lake Crillon."

CHAPTER 17
REORGANIZATION

"Welcome back, Juan. How was your vacation? Roy looked up from the maps on his desk as Juan entered the office. "Four weeks in the Caribbean must have been nice."

"Boss, I've almost forgotten how much I don't like snow anymore. The sun and sand were glorious. What are the maps for?"

"I've got a couple of trips to plan. Want to go?"

"If there are glaciers the answer is no. Who with?"

"Last week I visited Wallace Images. They have reorganized and consolidated their staff back into one building. They are leasing the space in the other building to several companies that use Wallace Imaging technology.

I met people from some of those companies. None of them were as gung ho as Raymond Wallace was but they did want some kind of outing. I thought a couple of weekend rock climbing trips would be good starters. No snow, yet."

"Okay, count me in. So what is happening at Wallace Images?"

"James is President. Marcy returned to Colorado. Eugene is acting head of Research and Development. Ian is acting head of Information Systems. Brad's secretary took over the Personnel Department. Michael is now Vice-President."

"I think Eugene will stay on in Research and Development. Ian will hire somebody to run the mainframe operations and make sure that the desktops are networked with the mainframe."

"So is what Raymond Wallace wanted to happen is happening?" Juan looked at some photos from the beginning of the Wallace Images trip hanging on the wall.

"I think so. Not the way he originally planned. The staff is working together and winning. Eugene used some of his inside contacts to get their languishing communication system on track and avoid bankruptcy.

"They plan to finish out the manufacturing activity and then return to straight R&D and idea brokering. The tenants in the buildings are autonomous but use Wallace Images computers and imaging technology. The technology is changing so rapidly it is difficult to settle on a product to manufacture. Developments will be licensed to companies that have existing products that can benefit from the Wallace technology. Eugene is really good at identifying companies that can benefit from using Wallace Image concepts and stimulating the thinking at those companies. He also has a lot of good ideas. He might not be as far out on the technology edge as Tom was but he is close."

"What do these new tenants do? The ones that want to take trips?"

"One of them is working on genome mapping and genome migration."

"Do they bite?"

"No, no, Juan," Roy laughed. "Genome research involves mapping human gene patterns. Heredity and all that stuff."

"What else?"

"Another company is in the oil exploration business and is interested in fossil DNA as an indicator of potential oil deposits. The company we are taking out is trying to simulate cultural migration using stochastic processes to see how known archeological sites fit possible migration patterns."

"Those are big words, boss. Let me know when I have too start."

"Juan, do you want to go to lunch? There is a new restaurant in the neighborhood that has the best Beef Stroganoff."

"Why, do you want it to do rain? Remember, it rained every time we had beef stroganoff on the trip; then there was an earthquake."

www.ingramcontent.com/pod-product-compliance
Lightning Source LLC
Chambersburg PA
CBHW071134170626
46809CB00002B/611